Pickin' Murder

(An Antique Hunters Mystery)

by

Vicki Vass

Betsy,

Merry Christmas!

thanks for the inspiration.

Love,

[illegible]

For information, email **Cozy Cat Press**,
cozycatpress@aol.com or visit our website at:
www.cozycatpress.com

COZY CAT PRESS

ISBN: 978-1-939816-72-6

Printed in the United States of America

Cover design by Paula Ellenberger
http://www.paulaellenberger.com/

1 2 3 4 5 6 7 8 9 10

A special thank you to the real Bradley at the Hermitage Hotel.

For always telling me I could follow my dreams, I'd like to dedicate this book to my mother, Joyce Vass.

Chapter One

Anne stood on the corner of the stage, just to the right of the large Marshall amps. Looking down, she admired the all-access pass hanging around her neck. She felt important. She *was* important, with a thousand eyes staring at her from the darkness, envying her. Dave Southwell, rising country star and Nashville hunk, gave her a wink as he took the stage.

"One, two, three," the drummer counted off, tapping his sticks together. The opening notes of "Young Hearts" started. Southwell slung his 1961 Fender Stratocaster over his shoulder. The Lake Placid blue guitar was worn and faded with a buckle rash across the back and pick scars across the front from where he'd beat each note out of the workhouse. He cradled the Shure microphone in both hands and sang the opening verse. The spotlights danced above him as he sang, reflecting blue, green and red. The audience sang along.

Standing next to Anne, CC turned her head away from the stage and lifted her camera to take pictures of the light rigging that hung high over the stage. "Anne, this is great. The rigging is made out of airplane quality aluminum so it's light but strong. This will be a perfect photo for my article for *Modern Steel*."

Anne turned a frustrated glance at CC. "That's fascinating but I'm trying to watch Dave." She turned her attention back to the stage, which was dark except for the halo spotlight over Dave's head. The motorized light spun around to illuminate Dave as he started his solo. With his back to the audience, he held his Strat up against his Marshall stack and hammered an *A* power chord. The Marshall's tubes glowed red hot, pushing their limits as the Celestion speakers filled the air. The crowd cheered. The halo spotlight swiveled, creaked, broke off, crashing down onto the young star's head. He crumpled to the ground. The audience was silent for a moment, and then screams broke out.

Still with her back to the stage, CC was explaining the strength of the light rigging to Anne who waved her off as she watched the terror unfold. CC continued talking until roadies yelled, "Clear the stage!" She stood silent as EMTs pushed past her. She stared in disbelief and then instinct kicked in. She snapped several photos before a large 300-pound roadie with a greasy black ponytail knocked her camera onto the ground. The badge around his neck read *Roger*.

"Hey, watch it!" CC said, picking the camera up and checking it for cracks.

"Off the stage!" he repeated. Half lifting them, he pushed them off the Naperville Last Fling stage and into the frantic crowd below.

Anne struggled to retain her footing. She turned around to face him. She half-heartedly held up her all-access pass to show the roadie. He grabbed it off her neck and escorted them to the guest room, a makeshift trailer. "We're not groupies," CC protested.

"Didn't think you were," he said as he slammed the door closed behind them.

CC eyed the room. All she saw was tall hair and short skirts. At 40 years old, she was probably old enough to be a very attractive older sister to many of these girls. Anne's Capri-flowered pants did not fit in nor did CC's plaid Bermuda shorts. "CC, do they realize who we are? Do they realize that Dave Southwell asked us to be here?" Anne asked.

"Anne, I think things have changed. I don't think Dave Southwell is going to be needing the microphone," CC said, checking out her camera.

Anne reached into her large orange Prada bag and retrieved the 1956 RCA microphone once used by Johnny Cash. They had discovered it at an estate sale of a former music producer. It had been buried deep in the basement behind some power tools.

A short while later, a Naperville police officer walked up to Anne and CC. "Ladies, can I ask you a few questions? Did you see what happened?" He looked at CC's all-access backstage pass. "Were you on stage when the accident happened?"

"Yes, we were guests of Mr. Southwell," CC said.

Anne interrupted, holding up the microphone. "We were commissioned to find this microphone for Dave Southwell. Johnny Cash used it in a Nashville recording. We found it. . ."

The officer interrupted her, "Who commissioned you?"

"We found it for our friend, Betsy. Her boyfriend is in the music industry," CC said.

Anne interrupted again, "We're the Spoon Sisters. That's the name of our business; we're not really sisters." Anne reached into her large orange Prada bag and handed him a business card, which read "Spoon Sisters, Antique Hunters." He took the card and jotted some notes down in his notebook.

Anne continued, "When he first went on stage, he walked by and gave me a wink. He recognized me because we had Face-timed each other after I found the microphone. He was very excited. We don't usually deal with musical instruments but this is an antique with a lot of history. Imagine Johnny Cash is holding this microphone in his hands in a small studio in Nashville. June is sitting on a stool in front of him.

Their eyes lock. He gives her a little crooked smile, and she blushes." Anne paused, closing her eyes for a second. "We help connect people with orphaned artifacts—you know—antiques." Anne took a large breath. "Is Dave okay?"

"I need to know only what you saw tonight," the officer said, not even trying to hide his annoyance.

"After Dave winked at me, he took the stage," Anne said. "The song started. It was his hit 'Young Hearts.' CC was bothering me, saying something about the lighting. I couldn't see around her so I missed what happened."

The officer turned to CC. "What about you?"

"My back was to the stage while I," CC paused, gave Anne a look and continued, "was bothering Anne."

"Is he okay?" Anne repeated.

The officer didn't answer her question, keeping his gaze on the notes he was scribbling in his notebook.

Anne pulled out her iPhone and brought up a picture of a man in a Chicago police uniform. "This is my boyfriend, the very tall and very British Detective Nigel Towers with the Chicago Police Department. Do you know him?"

The officer still didn't answer.

"We actually met when I helped him break a big case. You might have heard of it. The estate sale murders," Anne continued.

The officer still didn't answer.

"It happened on Chicago's North Shore about a year ago. It made all the local papers. It must have made it out to the burbs," Anne continued.

"Thank you. I've got your names and information," the officer said, closing his notebook and walking over to the group of groupies.

"I hope Dave's going to be okay," Anne said, turning to CC.

Anne and CC exited the trailer and watched the action on the stage. They heard the shrill of the sirens in the distance as they walked through the lingering crowd toward CC's Volkswagen microbus. The 1968 bus was a barn find, not much more than rust, nuts and bolts. After a year of tender loving care, CC had finally brought it back to life. She had become quite the shade tree mechanic since the divorce.

The early fall night was cool; the leaves were starting to turn. Naperville's Last Fling celebration marked the end of the summer festival season. Held at the city's Riverwalk, which led along the DuPage River, the festival attracted national musical acts with thousands of attendees. Walking past the food vendors, Anne was too concerned to be tempted by the pork chops on a stick or corndogs. *Wait, the funnel cake smelled good.* Covered in powdered sugar. *Maybe it would help her forget what happened.* She shuddered as she relived the image in her mind of Dave lying on the stage.

CC pulled her along. Voices chattered as they walked, many expressing disbelief, others crying. The festival air had turned sour. Anne and CC joined the march; they shared a common bond with these people. Dave's music had brought them together in joy, now it tore them apart in sorrow.

They trudged up the sled hill to wait at the crosswalk. At the top of the hill, CC turned around to look down at the stage. It was pitch black except for flashlights flickering like fireflies. The stage lights had been extinguished; CC feared the same for Dave.

When the light changed, Anne and CC followed the crowd across the street to the high school where CC had parked. The parking lot was packed. Cars were pulling haphazardly out of spaces and lining up in uneven, impatient rows.

"What do we do now?" Anne asked, getting in the car still clutching the microphone.

"Let's head home," CC said. She turned the key, and the VW came to life. CC backed out of the space and joined the line of cars. In her mind, the first line of "Young Hearts," and the last words Dave Southwell would ever sing repeated in her head, "I'm gonna live until I die."

Chapter Two

The day after the accident, CC stood in her basement darkroom. She rinsed the print paper in the developer, rocking it back and forth. Then she rinsed the print in water followed by the stop bath. When she was done, she squeegeed the paper and hung the print on the clothesline for drying. She hoped that she'd be able to use some of the pictures for her article on structural steel. For the past fifteen years, she had been reporting on steel for trade magazines. Not quite the career she had pictured when she'd graduated from journalism school, but it still paid the bills and required her to use her investigative skills. Sure, there wasn't a Pulitzer in her future, but her readers counted on her to be accurate and insightful.

With all the chaos from the onstage accident, she couldn't remember what she had shot. While the photos dried, she filled a mug with fresh-pressed French roast coffee, topped it with Redi-Whip and sat by the Ben Franklin stove in her sunroom, her favorite room in the house. The early fall morning was cool. The fire was warm. Bandit, her Australian shepherd, lay on her feet. He was better than the plushest slippers.

After a while, she went back to the darkroom and took the dried prints off the clothesline. She brought them to her drafting table in her sunroom, a find at a local furniture resale shop. After her divorce, CC had redone her house, decorating to her taste, scouring thrift stores and flea markets for bargains that needed a little love. She appreciated craftsmanship and the opportunity to bring these pieces back to life.

CC placed the pictures on her light box, a relic from her early days as a newspaper reporter. There were some great shots of the light rigging. In the background of one of the later shots, she could see Dave Southwell's body underneath the light. Southwell was obscured by the arm of Roger, the 300-pound roadie with the greasy ponytail. She was furious with him for knocking her camera down. Her 1947 Nikon lens was ruined. It was hard to find replacement parts for her model 6091 Nikon.

She took out her loupe to get a closer look. The resolution was beautiful, crisp. She preferred film to digital. It was more alive, more human. She found a perfect shot to illustrate her article. It was a close-up of the line of Par 64 lights attached to the lighting rig over Dave Southwell's head. That's when something caught her eye.

She lifted the picture up and put her loupe back to her eye. Several of the lights had wires with mountain climber hooks attaching them to the rigging. The four cans directly over Dave Southwell had the same wires but they were not attached. She Googled *stage lighting.* After watching several videos on YouTube, she realized that those wires were called safety wires and were used as a backup precaution. For some reason, the wires had not been attached properly.

Grabbing the pictures, she drove out to the Naperville Riverwalk. When she walked up the sled hill and to the stage, the crew was packing Dave Southwell's equipment. CC saw Roger, the roadie, supervising the evacuation. Naperville security stopped her before she could reach the stage. She pulled out her press pass that she carried everywhere. She flashed it at them and then threw it around her neck.

"Roger!" she yelled, running up to the stage.

He was sitting on a Marshall anvil steel case, smoking a cigarette. He turned as he heard his name.

CC climbed up the stage. "Roger, I'm CC. I was backstage yesterday."

He took another puff and gave her an uninterested look. "I know."

"I developed my photos." She pulled the 8 x 10 from her backpack. "These are the lights over Dave Southwell's head. The safety wires weren't attached. They could have saved his life."

He looked it over quickly. "I don't see it. "

CC pointed to the wires. "Look, you can tell they're not attached. They're next to the lights." She paused, reached back into her backpack, trying to find her loupe. "You have to look through a loupe."

Roger took a last drag of his cigarette, flicked it to the ground and stomped it out with his boot. "We checked all the lights before Dave came out." He shoved the photo back at her and then walked away.

CC stood stunned. She watched as a worker scrubbed the aluminum stage floor and the last remnants of Dave Southwell. She looked up at the lights but there was nothing there. The entire rigging had been dismantled.

Chapter Three

Dave Southwell's death shocked the country music world. A week had passed since the *Mayhem in Naperville* tragedy as Anne referred to it. She was still not able to get the picture out of her mind. The Spoon Sisters' blog's fans shared their grief, but life went on. Anne had to return to the serious work of antique hunting.

She arrived at CC's house early Saturday morning. The front of the suburban split-level was decorated with corn stalks, pumpkins, gourds and a scarecrow couple CC had made in her craft room. The scarecrow couple was very sad and coming apart at the seams. *Craft room*, Anne thought. *CC threw that word around kind of loosely.* Anne sat down on the cement bench that CC's ex husband had built, the only handyman project left standing. Scattered around it were orange mums in decorative planters.

Normally, Anne resented getting up this early, but weekends were a different story. Saturdays and Sundays were spent shopping—and not just any shopping—true antique hunting. On the weekends, Anne and CC scoured antique stores, estate sales, flea markets, garage and barn sales searching for items on their lists of *fan* requests. They went where the bargains were.

For the occasion, Anne was wearing her antique hunting uniform, a pair of flowered Capri pants once worn by 1960s Hollywood starlet Stevie Vann. The flowered pants had become a Spoon Sisters' symbol of empowerment, plus they looked damned good on her.

Since starting the Spoon Sisters' blog, their fan base had exploded. Hundreds of requests came in every week and Anne took a personal interest in each one. On a weekly basis, she scanned and mapped out their shopping expeditions, reading the classifieds, Craigslist and estatesales.net. She reviewed the photos and descriptions, comparing them against listings on eBay, Sotheby's and her own personal database, which was larger than both. She cataloged all her purchases in handwritten notebooks, which were organized by date, item, location and how much she had paid, also the estimated value. This was almost a full-time job. To keep up with the demand, she had switched her daytime job as a research chemist to part time. She had found her true calling—antique hunting.

CC and Bandit walked up behind her, disturbing Anne's thoughts. "Anne, you're early," CC said.

Anne jumped. "I was anxious to get started today. In fact, I couldn't sleep."

"How's Nigel? Did he like the poster?" CC asked after Anne's friend, the very tall and very British Chicago police detective Nigel Towers.

"He thought it was fabulous," Anne enthused, recalling Nigel's delight when she had given him an original Maltese Falcon movie poster. Nigel shared Anne's love of film noir.

CC opened the front door and took off Bandit's leash. She deposited it in a basket. Anne followed her into the house. "Sit down. I want to show you something," CC said.

Anne sat down at the dining room table, a 1960s-era Danish modern. Not Anne's taste, but it catered to CC's pragmatism and love of clean lines. Anne preferred her furniture more ornate.

CC pulled the photos out of her backpack and handed them to Anne. "What am I looking at?" Anne asked.

CC handed her the loupe. "Look closely at the overhead lights. Do you notice anything?"

Anne took a closer look through the loupe. "Not really."

"Look again." CC wondered if her imagination was playing tricks on her. She was starting to doubt her journalistic eye. "Check out the safety wires over Dave Southwell's head. They're not connected to the lights. If they were, it might have saved his life."

Anne pulled the loupe back up to her eye and examined the photo again. "I can kind of see it." She put the photo down on the table.

CC sat down next to her. "I went to the Riverwalk and showed it to Roger, the roadie who kicked us off the stage."

"What did he say about it?"

"He didn't see it either. He said all the lights were checked and secure."

"Obviously they weren't secure otherwise Dave would still be alive," Anne said.

"The official report says that the motorized halo light was not balanced correctly, and the weight pulled down the rest of the lights. I have a friend who works for the city of Naperville. She gave me a copy of the police report. Officially, they're calling it an accident." CC cradled her coffee cup.

"You don't feel it was?" Anne asked.

"After the year we had last year, I don't want to take anything at face value," CC said.

Anne agreed with her friend but wasn't sure what the next steps would be.

CC put the photos back in her backpack and stood up. "I'm going to make breakfast for us. You can map out our route for today."

While CC cut up onions and mushrooms and sautéed them in a pan, Anne sat at the kitchen table with a notebook and pen. She had a large Rand McNally atlas spread out on the table. "You know I have a GPS, right?" CC said over her shoulder.

"I hate that whiny voice. They're always yelling at me," Anne replied, using a compass to determine areas within a 50-mile radius of CC's home.

CC beat the eggs, added some cream and then the vegetables. She stirred them all together and put them in a cast iron skillet. When Anne wasn't looking, she added a dash of her ghost pepper mixture into the batter. CC's crop of hot peppers found its way into most of her meals. Even when dining out, she carried a small vial in her purse. As she was known to say, "It makes everything better." She put the frittata in the oven and then plopped some whole-wheat toast in the toaster.

When it was ready, she prepared some plates, adding strawberries with mint leaves and brought them over to the table. She poured them both a glass of fresh squeezed orange juice and coffee made from her authentic French press.

While they ate, Anne kept her eyes on her notebook and phone. She had several items she was watching on eBay. It was her primary leisure activity. She did very little buying online but considered it research.

When they were finished with their breakfast, they enjoyed their coffee in CC's 1960s era Frankoma coffee mugs. Anne, unable to contain herself any longer, burst out, "Can we go now? We have to be at the first sale before the doors open."

CC smiled. "What are we looking for today?"

"I combed through the list of requests you printed out for me and I cross referenced it with all the estate, garage, yard, rummage sales in the area this weekend, and I think our best bet is the Lake Forest Presbyterian Church rummage sale."

CC sighed. "Anne, you have to be kidding. Do you remember last year? Thousands of people, no parking and the lines. Oh, and what about the port-a- potty? What kind of church doesn't let you use their washroom? I don't remember reading anything in the Bible about port-a-potties."

"Just go before we get there," Anne said. "I know for sure at least ten items we're looking for will be there. The treasure room alone should have several sets of china including Rosenthal, Wedgwood or possibly Tiffany. And, there's a rumor that there's a Flora Danica china set. If I can find that at a good price, that alone is worth the trip. I'd sell Sassy for a Flora Danica salad bowl."

This was serious indeed, CC thought. If Anne was willing to part with her beloved white Persian over this china set, then it must truly be special.

As they reached downtown Lake Forest, the first signs for shuttle bus pick-up appeared. Parking was at a premium and Anne could already see people walking toward the church. She bit her nails, a childhood habit that had returned to her after the stress of the past year. "Anne, this is crazy. It's way too crowded," CC complained as they drove around looking for a parking space.

"Why don't we at least drive by the church and see how bad the lines are?" Anne said.

CC reluctantly agreed. They turned down the tree-lined street. The large parking lot across from the church was filled. The Lake Forest police officers were waving cars past. "Oh, dear," Anne said. That's when she caught a glimpse of periwinkle blue. "Stop! Stop the car, CC. Stop right now!" she yelled. She tried to jump out of the car but was restrained by the seatbelt. She stuck her head out the window and looked over the roof of the VW. Her worst fear was realized. In the small VIP parking lot behind the church, sat a periwinkle blue Aston Martin with the vanity plate, *Bets' Aston*. "Buttersworth!" she screamed, causing the birds in the trees to fly away and several passerby to turn their heads.

"Sit down," CC said as people honked behind them. "I have to move the car."

Anne managed to unbuckle her seatbelt and kick the door open with her foot. She exited the car while it was still in motion. "Just leave me here!" she shouted over her shoulder as she darted across the street, running towards the entrance. Her large orange Prada bag flew behind her trying to catch up. Cars squealed and swerved around her, the drivers yelling language not fit for church.

Pushing through the crowds, Anne ran up the staircase and down the narrow hallway. A sign in front of a classroom read *Treasure Room*. There were already nine people in line waiting for the door to open. Anne nervously poked her head left and right around the heads in front of her like a pigeon. As the door opened, she saw the back of a head with a perfect $300 coiffure rush in. *Buttersworth*, she thought.

When Anne finally entered the room, her gaze was immediately drawn to a low table. There it sat in all its glory, rim trimmed in pure gold, a five-piece place setting of Flora Danica. It would be hers. After her heart started beating again, she caught her breath and made her way to the setting. Laser focused, she did not see the manicured hand with a five-carat pink diamond engagement ring reaching for it.

The room stilled as Betsy Buttersworth turned with a smile holding the dinner plate in one hand and her vintage Hermes Birkin bag in the other. "Buttersworth!" Anne screamed. The stained glass church window might have rattled a bit.

"Hillstrom," was the reply from Anne's antique hunting nemesis, Betsy Buttersworth, no relation to the syrup but as always a very sticky problem for Anne. "It's been a while, Hillstrom."

Anne counted to ten in her head without realizing she was still moving her lips. When her blood pressure reached a manageable level, she said, "I came here today specifically for the Flora Danica set. It's number one on my request list for the Spoon Sisters blog."

Betsy listened respectfully trying not to smirk. She thought for a moment and handed it to Anne. "Well, then you must have it, mustn't you?"

Anne dropped the plate, thankfully recovering it when it was just an inch from the floor. She froze, holding it for a second and then rose slowly. "Buttersworth, why?"

"Anne, we're friends, aren't we? And friends help each other, don't they, Anne?"

"Yes, Betsy. Yes, they do," Anne's voice quivered, her pupils dilated.

"I want you to have this because it means so much to you and because it's so important to you. I, as your friend, want you to have this beautiful set of china."

"Here you are!" CC called out as she entered the room. "How could you have taken off like that?"

Betsy smiled at CC before walking away. Anne watched her, her mouth wide open, the china plate cradled in her arms.

"What was that all about?" CC asked Anne.

"Hell froze over," Anne replied.

"In church, Anne? Really?" CC looked at her. "Do you need more china?"

"It's number one on our list. It's the Flora Danica set I was telling you about. This could be worth $8,000, and they have priced it at $200."

"Are you sure it's not imitation? That's really a discounted price."

"It's not an imitation. That's real gold trim. Betsy let me have it."

"What do you mean Betsy let you have it?"

"She was holding it first and I told her how much it meant to me and she let me have it." Anne stared after Betsy who was holding up a silver vase. She could tell from here that it wasn't real silver-plate. Maybe she should warn her but, *unnh* she thought, shrugging her shoulders.

"Betsy? Betsy Buttersworth?"

"Yes." Anne pulled her Coach wallet out of her large orange Prada bag. It wasn't a Hermes but still a luxury item. Maybe a poor man's luxury item but luxury nonetheless. She gathered the twenties, singles and fives along with her baggie of change. She paid for the place setting and asked them to hold it for her while she walked around.

After an hour of wandering, she found CC in the designer clothing room in the basement trying on a pair of wide-wale corduroy pants. "No, those aren't for you," Anne said.

"You're going to talk about pants, are you?" CC gave a pointed look at Anne's flowered capris.

Anne plowed through the basket of scarves looking for a vintage Chanel or Vuitton, something worth her time, not these cheap polyester knockoffs. Down at the very bottom, she found a Burberry silk scarf in an original Nova Check pattern—navy, white and red checkers on a tan background. She held it up and slid it through her fingers. *This scarf found me,* she thought, *we are meant to be*. She wrapped it around her neck, unafraid that it would clash with her flowered pants.

She meandered into the game room where she found a vintage MET mahjong set, all original Bakelite and in its alligator briefcase. She estimated it to be a circa-1940 set. At $50, it was a steal. She could resell it for $250 or maybe $300 and there was a collector on her list looking for one. Over the past year, CC and Anne had scratched out a small profit by locating items for their fans. Anne struggled with the concept of only charging a *finder's fee* but CC made sure the small profit they made was fair to both them and the fans. As the list grew, so did the profits. Anne was hoping she could make the Spoon Sisters, Antique Hunters, her full-time career.

As she found and checked off more items, that possibility was becoming a reality. This room contained many items on the list. Arms overflowing, she went outside to the garden tent. It was crowded inside with people holding silk flowers, baskets, ceramic arts and yard art. She was drawn to a Japanese cricket house. This would be perfect for CC's koi pond. She grabbed it before another woman could snatch it up. Then she picked up a brass planter, looked it over, and set it down. It was a bullet atomic planter, solid brass with a turquoise interior. *Mid-century modern*, Anne thought, *not her style*. Then she thought about it again but the cricket woman was now holding it. "Excuse me, I was looking at that first," Anne said.

"I didn't see you holding it," The cricket woman said, turning to talk to her friend so her back was facing Anne.

"Hmmph," Anne said, thinking about it for a moment. "That's okay; you can have it. By the way, it's overpriced." Anne walked away, feeling good about herself.

She carried the rest of her items to the long wooden counter where the cash registers were and paid for her purchases. She waited by the front doors for CC who came out bearing two large shopping bags. "What'd you find?"

"I got an early F-body Nikon and some lens filters. Look at these cigar boxes," CC said. "They are from 1950's Cuba. I am going to make everyone boxes for Christmas this year."

Anne thought about CC's boxes. They were decoupage, glued with images from vintage catalogs, magazines and yearbooks. More of a hodgepodge than art. Another project from her craft room but she didn't want to discourage her friend. "Anything else?" Anne asked, struggling under the weight of her bags.

"I bought the pants. I think I look good in them. I bought something for Tony." She reached into one of the bags and pulled out a white captain's cap.

"That's nice. Have you spoken to him lately?"

"We talked on the phone a couple nights ago. He's been busy getting ready for Italy."

They boarded the shuttle bus, balancing their bags on their laps. The bus was crowded and jostled along the road. Anne cradled the china like a newborn. When they reached the parking lot, they found CC's 1968 VW bus blocked in behind a Mercedes and Lexus. "We'll have to wait," CC said.

"I'm not waiting." Anne got out of the car and walked over to the police officer who was directing traffic. Minutes later, cars were being moved. "I showed them the picture of Nigel in his dress uniform. I might have said, my husband, Detective Nigel."

"Anne, you're really bad," CC said. "Are you hungry? Do you want to stop for lunch?"

Lunch, Anne thought, *would be nice but she still had a long list of places to stop before heading home*. "We don't have time for lunch. I've brought some turkey sandwiches." She reached into her large orange Prada bag and pulled out two foil wrapped packages. She handed one to CC.

By the end of the day, Anne was exhausted and broke. When they reached CC's house, she barely had enough energy to carry her bags to her car. It took a while for her to fit everything into the already overcrowded Mercury Mystique.

CC, seeing Anne shuffling to her car, asked, "Do you want to come in for dinner? I can whip something up."

At the click of the key, Bandit ran to greet them at the door. Anne barely acknowledged Bandit and plopped down on the sofa. She kicked off her sensible penny loafers and rubbed her aching arches. "CC," she yelled over her shoulder as CC went into the kitchen. "I was thinking about the Flora Danica. What are the chances I'm ever going to find a set like that for a price like that?"

CC grabbed some fresh shrimp from her fridge, cleaned them and put them in a saucepan with lemon juice, garlic and olive oil. "Anne, you're not thinking about keeping them, are you?" she asked while chopping lettuce.

"I'm just saying, would it be the worst thing in the world if just this one time I kept something on the list for myself. Let's face it, we're never going to find everything on the list. I'm willing to try, of course, and I enjoy helping people out. I enjoy hunting for treasures but don't you feel like we deserve a little happiness, too." Anne studied the plate. "This plate makes me happy."

CC half listened as the oil started sizzling. She placed two halves of Romaine lettuce brushed with olive oil, Parmesan cheese, salt and pepper on a stovetop grill. She was helping Anne keep to her low carb diet. She turned down the pan with the shrimp and added a splash of vermouth. As the liquor cooked off, she went down to her cellar and selected a bottle of her homemade cherry wine that she had put up earlier in the season.

She brought Anne a glass. "Why don't we eat and then we'll talk about it?"

Anne sipped tentatively. "This is really good. Where'd you get this?"

"The backyard," CC replied. "My cherry trees. It's an old family recipe. Actually very simple. You mash up the cherries, add sugar and water, some yeast and then let it ferment. The trick is to pick the cherries at just the right time when they're at their sweetest. I had a really good crop of cherries this year."

Between being tired and thinking about the china, Anne blocked CC out. She often had selective hearing when it came to her friend. CC was a wealth of knowledge when a penny's worth would do.

CC placed the romaine on the plate and put the shrimp on top of it. She sprinkled feta on it, garnished it with fresh herbs and her homemade blueberry vinaigrette. She poured more wine and sat at the table.

Anne sat across from her, with her phone near her side. The prices on her eBay watch list items were climbing and probably out of her price range but it was still fun to look. "What's going on with you and Nigel?" CC asked.

"He asked me to go to Galena for the weekend. You know I love Galena. It's just blocks and blocks of antique shops, cute cafes and bed and breakfasts." Anne pictured the quaint town in her mind's eye.

"Anne, I don't think he wants to go for the antiquing. I think he wants to spend quality time alone with you," CC reprimanded her.

"I know that. It's just I'm uncomfortable with being with him in that way."

"What do you mean that way?" CC asked.

"In a romantic way, you know," Anne speared a shrimp with her fork and took a big gulp of her wine.

"Anne, you've been dating him for a year now."

"I wouldn't exactly call it dating." Anne paused. "I like him but I don't know if I like him that way."

"Anne, he's not asking you to get married. He's asking you to go to Galena for a weekend."

"I'm afraid if I say *yes* he's going to get the wrong idea. Don't get me wrong. I think he's attractive, sweet, funny, but I don't have those feelings for him. I wanted to but it isn't happening."

"I think if that's the way you feel, you should let him know. I've seen the way he looks at you."

"CC, I'm afraid if I tell him, I'm going to lose him. He means a lot to me. I want him to be my friend. I enjoy his company but I don't feel that spark that knocks me off my heels." Anne looked at her plate and moved her food around.

CC knew what Anne was talking about because she felt that spark with Tony. After dinner, CC brought up her computer and went to her blog site. "Anne, you never wrote your post for this week."

"I'm too tired to think about that now. I'll do it tomorrow when I'm fresh."

"Dear Friends," CC typed, "Anne and I are back from the Lake Forest Presbyterian Church rummage sale. It was crowded as always."

Anne put her fingers up to her mouth and said, "Shhh. Don't tell them about the plates. I haven't decided yet."

"You know they can't hear us, right?" CC returned to typing and jumped at the buzzing coming from her computer. "Anne, I have a Face-time coming in. It's Tony."

"Do you want me to leave?" Anne asked.

"Don't be silly." CC straightened her hair, put on lipstick and checked herself in the mirror. She sat back down. A handsome man with salt and pepper hair and a weatherworn face appeared on her iMac. "CC, are you there?" Tony asked.

"Hi, Tony, can you see me now?" She waved at him.

"Yes."

"You look great."

CC blushed.

"I'm here, too." Anne waved from behind CC.

"I finished the ship. If I want to sail it back to Italy this year, I have to leave soon. Look, I'll show you." Holding his iPhone, he gave her a panoramic view from the dock.

"She's beautiful, Tony." CC hesitated a minute before asking, "Couldn't you have someone else sail it back?"

"The agreement I made with the buyer included delivery and stated that I would hand deliver it. I've spent the past 18 months working on her," he paused. "I want to take her out on the open sea. Let's meet for dinner tomorrow and we can talk."

"Sounds good, Tony." She clicked off.

"Why does he have to move back?" Anne asked.

"It's a good opportunity. His mentor at the shipyard is retiring and he wants Tony to take over for him. Tony was his apprentice for ten years. He learned everything about restoring yachts from him. I understand the allure of working on beautiful works of art and living in southern Italy."

"Well, CC, like you were quick to tell me, I think you should let Tony know your feelings."

"Well, Anne, if he asks me to go I think I'll go."

"What about the Spoon Sisters? What about me? Are you going to leave me behind?"

"Let's cross that bridge when we get to it." CC looked at her phone. "This is strange." She had a text from Betsy Buttersworth. "Betsy wants us to come for brunch tomorrow."

"She's not getting the plates." Anne crossed her arms over her chest.

CC sighed. "Let's go and see what she wants."

Chapter Four

They arrived at Betsy's historic Frank Lloyd Wright prairie home in the near west Chicago suburb of Oak Park. The Sunday morning gawkers with their walking tour headphones stopped politely to admire the brass plaque that adorned Betsy's front door. The short walk up to the building was lined with fall mums. Anne hesitated halfway up the stairs. "CC, you're sure this is a good idea? Every time we get involved with Buttersworth, something bad happens." Anne was decked out for brunch in a silk shantung two-piece suit, white gloves and a large straw hat with a pink ribbon. CC was wearing the wide wale corduroys with a turtleneck. She was carrying a bottle of her homemade cherry wine.

Before Anne could change her mind, CC rang the doorbell. Moments later, Betsy Buttersworth appeared wearing a vintage Halston dress and saltwater pearls. She smiled at CC and then looked Anne up and down. The smile faded. "Come in." She held the door open for CC and let it close slightly, rubbing against Anne as she walked through, pretending not to notice.

The inside of Betsy's home was as pristine as the exterior. Everything in it was era appropriate. FLW, as Betsy referred to him, would have approved. "Ladies, we're going to have brunch in the sunroom. I have it all set up. Please follow me back."

As they walked on the slate tile, the stained glass window in the upstairs landing stole Anne's gaze. The Sunday morning sun was shining through, painting the floor with reds, blues, greens and ambers silhouetting the oak stairs like a pulpit in a Baptist church. Anne imagined FLW standing at the pulpit preaching the gospel of prairie design. "Hillstrom, are you coming?" Betsy said from the hallway that narrowed through the kitchen and into the sunroom.

Oh, last names again, Anne thought. That was one thing about Buttersworth that really irritated her. She'd known Buttersworth since they were kids, yet Betsy refused to call Anne by her first name. It was always *Hillstrom*, like *Hillstrom* was an insult.

Following Betsy and CC into the sunroom, Anne saw the beautifully set table. It was adorned with vintage French linens and a lace embroidered tablecloth covering the leather top round oak table.

"Please sit down, ladies."

Betsy walked over to the sideboard and retrieved a crystal pitcher full of orange juice. She filled three Lalique champagne flutes with Dom Perignon and a splash of orange juice. She sat down and neatly creased her dress. "Let's have a toast, shall we? To old friends, the best kind of friend."

Anne tentatively sipped. She kept waiting for Buttersworth to bring up the china. She knew that's what this was all about. What else could it be? She couldn't contain herself anymore. The pressure was too much; the waiting, the worrying, the stress level was unbearable. "You can't have the china," she blurted out, and then downed her Mimosa like it was a true Swedish toast.

"Hillstrom, what china are you talking about?"

"Okay, Buttersworth, you can stop with the games. You know you brought us here to try to take back the china from the rummage sale. It's not going to happen. You had your chance, you passed on it, it's mine, end of story." Anne set her glass down on the table with a thud and stood up.

"Oh, Anne, you're a riot," Betsy said with a noticeably fake laugh. "I wanted to wait until after we ate to tell you why I asked you here. We can talk about it now." Betsy twisted the ring on her finger so the stone was facing up and waved it in the air. The light was blinding. "Steven's asked me to marry him."

"Oh, congratulations," CC said, admiring the ring. "It's beautiful."

"It's very big," Anne said, giving it a glance.

"Steven will be moving to Chicago," Betsy said, accenting her point with hand motions. "We've been flying back and forth, making time between our busy schedules."

"Do you have a wedding date?" CC said, tapping Anne's foot under the table.

"Not quite yet. We're still working out the details."

"That's why you want the china," Anne said.

"Oh, Anne, you are funny. I don't need your china. What I would like is to commission you to help me with a project. I'm converting my coach house in back to a studio for Steven. I envision a combination office and music room. I would like to keep it authentic like the main house. Early 1900s antiques but with a music theme like vintage guitars, radios, microphones, posters. I want a lot of Nashville memorabilia. I want him to feel at home."

"Why us?" Anne asked, biting at her fingernail.

"Steven was very impressed that you were able to find that microphone for Dave Southwell." Betsy paused. "What a tragedy. Dave was signed to one of Steven's subsidiaries. Anyway, I'd like to hire you exclusively to furnish my coach house. Between planning the wedding and my charity work, I don't have time to do it myself. Besides, we have a history.

You know what I like and I trust your eye. It's going to be a surprise for Steven so I'm under a time constraint. I'd like to get the whole house done before Steven is back from Nashville. I have several leads from various sources. Some antique dealers, some musicians who might want to sell some of their equipment. It'll give you a good start. Of course, I'll pay you a hefty commission."

"Betsy, we'd love to help you but we both have full-time jobs," CC said. "We couldn't take off that much . . . ."

"Don't be silly," Anne interrupted, jumping at the chance of an adventure like this. "Of course, we can. This is a great opportunity for the Spoon Sisters to grow our business. And, of course, we want to help Betsy. We're all old friends."

"Thank you, Anne, I'm glad you feel that way."

CC hesitated. "I guess I can file my stories from Nashville just as easily as from Chicago. I'll have to work it out with my boss but it's a possibility."

Betsy refilled all three glasses with just a touch of orange juice and a larger splash of champagne. "Here's to the Spoon Sisters and a successful hunt!" she declared.

Chapter Five

CC arrived at the Italian Village, a Chicago landmark. Tony was already waiting. He had reserved a special booth in a quiet corner on the second floor. The twinkling white string lights wrapped around the booth, creating a romantic atmosphere. Tony stood up to greet CC as she reached the top of the stairs. He was wearing the sport coat he had worn the first time they saw each other on the Metra train over a year ago. It made her smile to see that he remembered that day. A glance from a stranger had turned into something more.

He kissed her cheek and handed her a single red rose. He escorted her back to the booth. He sat down and she sat across from him. Before he could speak, the waiter came by. "Can I get you a drink?"

Tony ordered a fine bottle of wine in Italian. "I love this place," CC said as she gazed around the room. "Did you know that this restaurant is almost 90 years old? Imagine we could be sitting in a booth where Al Capone ate. Frank Sinatra had his wedding celebration here."

"That's very interesting, CC." Tony took her hand in his. "I wanted to talk with you about Italy. When I sail the Baglietto back to Italy, I'm going to take Angelo's offer. I've found a villa overlooking the Mediterranean close to the shipyard."

CC looked down and broke off a piece of bread. "I understand. You're a master craftsman. These beautiful boats are your life's work. It's a wonderful opportunity. I'm very happy for you."

"It's been a tough decision. I have a lot to leave behind." Tony paused and sipped his wine. "I've come to really care about you. In fact, I love you. I don't want to return to Italy without you."

"Are you asking me to marry you?"

Tony's silence was CC's answer. "It's not that I don't want to share my life with you. I do. After my wife died, I didn't want to continue on. As much as you've brought joy into my life, I still have that sorrow that stays with me. I don't know if it's possible to love twice in a lifetime the same way I loved her, but I'd like to try and find that kind of love with you."

"Tony, I love you, too. I think moving to Italy with you and sharing your life and your boats would be wonderful." She paused. "You're asking me to leave everything I know behind to take a chance at a life with you and you're not even sure that you can commit to me. That's something I can't do."

"Where does that leave us?" he asked.

"That leaves us with enjoying dinner tonight and whatever time we have together before you have to leave." CC felt an aching in her heart as she pictured saying goodbye to him.

Chapter Six

Early Monday morning, Anne waited on the front porch of her Chicago brick bungalow for CC. Surrounding her was the pile of suitcases and bags that contained her essentials. It was day one of the Buttersworth hunt. Anne waved to Grandma Pat sweeping her front sidewalks. Pat Irwin, *Grandma Pat* as Cedar Avenue knew her, was the neighborhood watch. She was responsible for bringing the garbage cans up, delivering newspapers from the curb to the doorstep and keeping an eye out for the neighborhood. Pat waved at Anne and walked up her front stairs.

"Anne, how are you? You're up early."

"CC and I have a special project we're working on," Anne said. "We want to hit the highway before traffic gets bad. We're heading to Nashville."

"Nashville? Why Nashville?"

"We're going to look at some vintage guitars and antiques. We've been commissioned by a client," Anne said. "Pat, would you sit for minute? I have something to ask you."

Pat leaned her broom against the swing and sat in the white wicker rocker next to Anne. "Anne, if it's about your leaves, I noticed you haven't had a chance to get to them. I'd be more than happy to clean them up."

"No, Pat, that's not it. I might be gone for a couple weeks. I was wondering if you could keep an eye on the house and maybe watch Sassy."

"I love Sassy. I'd be glad to do that. She's a sweetheart."

Sassy, the white Persian, watched the whole conversation from the bay window. She knew they were talking about her but wasn't sure what they were saying. She got tired of watching and returned to her work with the fuzzy mouse.

"Anne, I haven't seen that nice very tall and very British detective Nigel coming around much anymore. How are things?" Pat asked.

Anne's excitement turned to sadness. Grandma Pat placed a hand on her knee. "Are you okay?"

"Well, Pat, Nigel asked me to go away with him for the weekend and I turned him down. I really care for him, but I don't feel that way about him. I don't feel the spark."

"Dear, I was married for 50 years and I had that spark from the day I met Gino, and I still feel it today even though he's gone. If you don't feel that way about Nigel, he's not the right man for you."

CC pulled up in the light green and pearl two-tone VW bus and honked. Anne gave Grandma Pat a hug and ran down the stairs, carrying her large orange Prada bag and lugging her large roller bag down the stairs. She shoved it in the back of the VW bus and then went back for the rest.

"What is all this?" CC asked from the window. "I told you to only bring what you needed."

"These are my essentials." Anne shoved the other two suitcases and overnight bag into the back. "You never know what you'll need. It could rain, be hot or snow in the mountains."

After leaving Bandit with CC's brother, the Spoon Sisters hit the road. They drove out of Illinois into Indiana on the crowded tri-state toll way. "Where is everyone going?" Anne said, unfolding the Rand McNally atlas. "I've marked off a few interesting antique stores along the way where we can stop."

"I already have the route plotted out. It's in the GPS," CC said, turning on the navigation system. "We're going to make a little detour on the way. We're going to stop in Corbin, Kentucky," CC added.

"Why are we stopping there?"

"I read an article in *Guitar Player* magazine."

"CC, when did you start reading *Guitar Player* magazine?"

"I picked it up at the dentist office. The cover read *steel guitar*, and it caught my eye. There's this old steel guitar player named Scooter Muscarello. I guess he was a big sideman back at the Grand Ole Opry in the early 1960s. He played in a lot of bluegrass bands. He had quite a collection of guitars. He passed away recently and his granddaughter is planning an estate sale."

"Oh, that sounds promising; when's the sale?"

"I contacted her and she's going to let us come look before the sale."

"That's a good find, CC." Anne was impressed. She couldn't have done better herself.

"And since we're in the area, we can stop at Cumberland Falls for the night. I made reservations for us."

"Why?" Anne was not an outdoorsy type.

"To see the waterfall. It's been called the Niagara of the South or the Great Falls. The falls are 68 feet high and 125 feet wide with an average water flow of 3600 cubic feet per second."

Anne's eyes glazed over. "And? And? And?"

"I'm hoping we can get some pictures of the moon bow," CC said.

"Moon bow?" If possible, Anne's eyes glazed even more.

"On nights when the moon is full and the sky is clear, a moon bow appears. It's a white arc starting at the base of the falls and covers the entire length. It's the only one in the western hemisphere." At the look on Anne's face, CC added, "We're just spending one night and then we're on to Nashville."

For lunch, they stopped at Cousin's hamburger restaurant located on the outskirts of Louisville, Kentucky. "I heard about this place on the Food Network. Best hamburgers in the Midwest, forty different toppings, everything made fresh," CC said.

They sat down and ate. Anne had the double cheeseburger piled high with Merkt's cheese, onions, pickles, bacon, and a real vanilla milkshake. To accompany it, she had French fries three ways, bacon, sour cream and melted cheddar cheese. CC had the same.

Heading back to the VW, Anne nibbled on her fresh-baked chocolate chip cookie.

The flatlands of Illinois had given way to the rolling hills of Kentucky as they drove along the Blue Ridge Parkway. Heading off the highway into Corbin, they followed the winding road that was bordered by tall hemlocks and pines soaring 100 feet overhead. CC pulled the VW bus into the circle driveway in front of the DuPont Lodge. "You know, Anne, this was named after T. Coleman DuPont. He grew up here and gave the land to the state for a forest preserve."

Anne nodded as she stared at the rustic lodge. When she exited the VW, she saw the first of many bright yellow "Beware of Bear" signs. She pulled her large orange Prada bag closer to her. Walking inside, she found a large stone fireplace that was the centerpiece of the great room. It was surrounded by knotty pine bookshelves. Anne ran to the observation deck, which looked out over the Cumberland River while CC checked them in.

After bringing their overnight bags to their room, CC grabbed her camera and hiking shoes. She looked at

Anne who was lounging on the bed, reading one of the guidebooks she had picked up. "Are you coming?"

"I might stay here and rest."

"Anne, it's only a half-mile walk."

Anne grabbed her large straw hat and her bag and slowly followed CC out of the room. She swatted at mosquitoes as they walked along the path. Sweat dripped off her brow; she was definitely not made for the outdoors. Passing by the gift shop, Anne gave it a longing glance. Leaving it behind, she trudged behind CC.

While they walked, CC took pictures and nodded *hello* at other tourists. They stood at the top of the waterfall looking down. The waterfall was massive; the mist lofted up, cooling CC's brow. Anne was still hot and fanned herself with the bear-warning pamphlet. "What's over there?" CC pointed at a wood sign. It read "Lower Observation Area."

"Let's go." CC rushed down the steep uneven stairs, Anne followed behind.

When they reached the bottom, it split off in two directions. They took the path that split to the right. It was a single file stone walkway. On one side of the walkway, jagged rocks dropped off a hundred feet; on the other side was the edge of the cliff with more jagged rocks poking out.Anne felt surrounded. She also felt concerned that something was going to jump out at her from under the rocks. She was not a nature lover. She swatted at the flies and mosquitoes that buzzed around her.

When they reached the semicircular observation area, the sun was just setting. They climbed up the steps to the viewing area which was crowded with people pushing up against the railing to get a good look at the falls. As the sun set, the moon rose and so did the beautiful moon bow through the mist. "Anne, this is what we came here for." CC wiggled her way to the corner of the viewing deck next to the rocks. She had to stretch way over the railing to look around to get a good shot of the moon bow. She climbed up on the railing and straddled it.

Anne stood at the back of the crowd. She couldn't get a good view of the moon bow. She was hot, sticky and she really didn't care. Her feet ached and she was tired. This wasn't part of her game plan. Then she heard a scream. She stood on tiptoe and looked over a tall man's shoulder. People were frantic trying to reach over the railing to rescue CC who was dangling, clutching the support bracket under the railing with one arm. She was suspended a hundred feet over the crashing water.

Anne pushed her way through the crowd. "CC, my God, someone get help!"

A man stuck his arm through the bottom of the railing trying to reach for her, but she was too far away. CC's legs dangled, supported by only her arms.

"CC, hang on! They've sent for the park rangers!" Anne called after her.

"Anne, I'm slipping. I can't hang on!" CC's words came out in quick gasps. She could feel her grip slipping.

Anne looked around for anything, anyone to help her best friend. Dumping the contents of her large orange Prada bag on the ground, she found what she was looking for—her iconic vintage Burberry plaid silk scarf. She tied one end to the railing and flung the other down toward CC. "CC, grab on!" she yelled down to her friend.

"It'll never hold!"

"Of course, it will; it's Burberry!"

CC grabbed the scarf with her free hand and wrapped it around her wrist. The man, who had been trying to help, grabbed the scarf and pulled her up. Several people grabbed onto her and lifted her over the top of the railing. CC sat on the ground, catching her breath, her heart was still pounding.

"Are you all right? What happened?" Anne knelt down beside her and put her arm around her friend.

"I was trying to get a better angle of the falls and the moon bow. I sat on the edge of the railing. I was really careful."

"CC, that's so dangerous! How could you?"

"Anne, somebody pushed me."

"Who would push you?"

"I don't know if it was intentional. There was a lot of people crowding to see the moon bow." CC shook it off.

"The important thing is you're okay."

The park rangers arrived along with an emergency kit. CC stood up. "I'm fine. Really; I'm fine. No cuts or bruises. It was just an accident."

"Let us take you back to the lodge, ma'am," the ranger said, leading her and Anne to an all-terrain vehicle.

After examining CC, the girls were left sitting in front of the lodge's roaring stone fireplace, sipping their hot chocolate. Anne took off her shoes and massaged her aching feet.

When Anne had finished her second cup of hot chocolate with extra marshmallows, she turned to CC who had been sitting quietly, staring at the flames. "CC, are you okay to continue? Do you want to go home?"

"Anne, it was just a careless accident. I was being reckless. I will be more careful in the future," CC said. "You know the interesting part is I was able to hang by one arm for several minutes. All those pushups at the Glen Ellyn gym, shoulder pull-ups and the yoga are really paying off. You might want to think about joining."

"No, I think I'll avoid putting myself in situations where I need to dangle 100 feet over a waterfall." Anne paused. "I think that's the best exercise plan for me. Can we go eat now?"

Anne and CC walked into the lodge's restaurant. It resembled the cafeteria of a summer camp. One side was dedicated to a large buffet with fried catfish, hush puppies, salad bar and desserts. Anne perused the desserts before they sat at a table that had a view of the Cumberland River. She couldn't wait to try the banana pudding.

CC studied the menu. She was starving after her ordeal and was looking forward to trying a local specialty. "Anne, what are you going to have?"

"I think I'm going to try the buffet," she said.

When the waitress came over, Anne ordered the buffet and went to fill her plate. Balancing it carefully, she went back to their table. CC was not there.

Inside the lodge's kitchen, CC watched the chef as he prepared the Hot Brown, a famous Kentucky specialty. He layered turkey and roast beef over a slice of toast. He then poured the fresh cheese sauce, a combination of cream, butter and white cheddar cheese, on top of the meats. "This is fabulous," CC said as she sampled the cheese sauce.

Then the chef decorated it with a slice of crisp bacon, salt and pepper and a sprinkle of Parmesan cheese. He put it in the broiler. When it was crisp and browned, he put the sandwich on a plate and handed it to CC. "Thank you so much for showing me your recipe," she said. "Do you mind if I share this recipe on my blog?"

"Not at all, Miss CC," the chef said.

Bearing the plate in her hand, CC went back to the dining room and her table where Anne was plowing through her second plate of catfish and hush puppies. "Where were you? I was worried."

"The chef showed me how to make a Kentucky Hot Brown. It's a classic sandwich." Before picking up her knife and fork, CC reached into her purse and pulled out her ghost pepper mixture. She sprinkled some on the sandwich. "It makes everything better," she told Anne.

Later in their room, CC sat down at the desk and pulled out her iPad mini with its Zag keyboard. "Dear friends," she typed on her blog. "Today, Anne and I started our excursion for our first antique hunting commission. We stopped at Cumberland Falls and saw the moon bow rise over the waterfall. It was an amazing sight.

After that, Chef Alfred was kind enough to teach me how to make a Kentucky classic, the Hot Brown sandwich. He said I could share the recipe with you so here it is."

Chapter Seven

Following a good night's sleep, the Spoon Sisters headed to Corbin, a short drive from the falls. Scooter Muscarello's farm was on the outskirts of town—mostly everything was on the outskirts of town in Corbin. The new ranch home was situated on ten acres, next to a small lake. There was a horse barn with two palominos prancing along the split rail fence. The animals raced CC's VW bus as she pulled up the driveway. On the front porch was sitting Ellie Muscarello, Scooter's granddaughter. She was an attractive, 40-year-old blonde with her hair tied back tight in a ponytail, wearing jeans, riding boots and a flannel shirt. The morning air was cool and crisp. The oak and maple trees that surrounded the ranch were already orange and red, and the leaves were starting to fall.

As Anne and CC got out of the bus, the leaves crinkled under their feet. Anne took a big whiff of the fresh air and caught the whiff of the horses. She gagged.

CC was first up the short steps to the wraparound porch. "Ellie, I'm CC. Thank you so much for having us out," she said as she reached out her hand and shook Ellie's. "This is my friend and partner, Anne."

"Welcome! You must be the Spoon Sisters. After we spoke, I looked up your blog and read it. I really enjoyed it."

"Thank you, it's a lot of work but we love it," Anne said. CC shot her a look.

"I think my grandfather would have enjoyed it also. He was a collector and a picker." Ellie opened the screen door. "Why don't you come in? Can I get you some coffee?"

"That would be great," Anne said.

"Would you like some Danish?"

Before she could finish, Anne interrupted. "Danish? What kind of Danish?"

CC gave her a concerned look.

Anne stopped and said. "No, thank you; we just had breakfast."

The living room was packed full of guitar cases, record albums, old newspapers and sheet music. After handing Anne and CC mugs full of steaming hot coffee, Ellie said, "You can see there's a lot to look through. Grandpa Scooter collected musical instruments his whole life. He still played at age 91. Some of the older guitars and banjos he left to the Grand Ole Opry Museum. He played with Patsy Cline, Loretta Lynn, Hank Williams."

"That's quite a pedigree of stars," CC said.

"Let me show you some pictures." Ellie pulled out a stack from underneath a tower of record albums. CC looked through the black and white 8 x 10 photographs. "That's my grandfather." Ellie pointed him out. In the picture was a lanky good-looking man playing a lap steel guitar on the Ryman stage. There was another picture of Scooter standing next to Minnie Pearl.

"These are wonderful," CC said. "Would you consider selling any of them?"

"There are hundreds of them. I've got more boxes in the pole barn. I guess I could part with some of the ones I know that I have duplicates of."

"They will be going to a good home as I was telling you on the phone. Our client is acquiring collectibles for her fiancé, Steven Kendall."

"Oh, I've heard of him," Ellie said.

"He's from Nashville. Betsy, our client, is a wonderful collector. Anything we buy will be appreciated and taken care of," Anne said.

"Grandpa Scooter would want his things to go to a good home. He'd want people to see them and enjoy them. I don't have enough room at my house for anymore of his stuff. I've picked through what meant the most to me. My two boys are musicians—one plays drums, the other guitar. They picked what they wanted already. Grandpa Scooter didn't have a lot of money and he wanted to make sure both my boys had a good education. My oldest boy Kevin has been accepted to Berkley and my younger boy Peter is in his second year at Vanderbilt. All the money from the estate sale will pay for their education."

"That's wonderful that your grandfather could leave that legacy to your boys," CC said.

After looking through the crowded basement and making a pile of items, including the pictures, CC and Anne paid Ellie and loaded everything onto the bus. "Thank you so much," CC said to Ellie.

They got into the bus. "Where to now?" CC asked. Anne pulled out her large atlas along with several coupon books that she had picked up at the rest area.

"There's an antique mall in Hickory. We should stop," Anne said.

"Hickory what?"

"Actually, Hickory, North Carolina."

"We have to go through the Smoky Mountains to get there."

"That's great. I've never been through the Smoky Mountains. You can get some pictures there," Anne said.

CC hesitated. "It is supposed to be beautiful. I could get a lot of great shots."

Chapter Eight

From Corbin, they headed south on I-75. There was a slight drizzle as they got on the highway. As they drove, CC gave a history lesson. "You know, Anne, at one time North America and Africa were connected with the Appalachians being the center of the two continents." She paused. "They're actually from the same chain of mountains in Morocco known as Little Atlas. This mountain range, known as the central Pangaean, extends into Scotland. Isn't it amazing to think how at one time the whole planet was one big continent?"

Slightly listening to CC, Anne looked out her window watching the beautiful brown, green and red slate and granite canopy of rocks that were cut through the mountains to make the highway. Each curve brought a new vista more beautiful than the one before. The mountains, the luscious pines, the jagged rocks.

A rainbow appeared capping one of the mountains to its sister. Eagles danced overhead like they were following the VW. The rain started again. Anne could feel the VW accelerating as it descended down the highway. A sign warned *Nine Percent Incline*. Anne gripped the armrest. "CC, don't you think you should slow down a bit?"

"We're fine, Anne."

A Peterbilt semi- flew past in the left lane, spraying water, blinding CC temporarily as the wiper blades struggled to keep up. CC slowed down a bit as she felt her microbus hydroplane. "CC, slow down!" Anne felt her breakfast turn over in her stomach. She closed her eyes as if she were on a roller coaster.

When they reached the foothills of the Smoky Mountains, they followed the signs that read Great Smoky Mountain Parkway. The VW bus strained as it did the slow 30-minute climb up to Smoky Mountain National Park. CC turned in at the first vista point. "I'm going to walk around and take some pictures. Are you coming?"

"I think I will conserve my energy for the antique store," Anne said, thumbing through the visitor's guide.

The sun peeked out. CC walked along the bridge that jutted over the mountains. Eagles screeched overhead. A sea of orange and red blanketed the valley. The fall air was crisp and smelled like fresh pine. She wondered where Tony was at that moment. *Probably somewhere halfway between here and Italy. Was he thinking about her?*

She took a picture of the wooden sign that marked the *Free Speech* area that had been designated by Franklin Roosevelt who had dedicated the park. Walking back toward the car, she wondered why Anne was sitting in the driver seat. Anne turned and gave her a horrified look, a piece of her ham sandwich hanging out of her mouth. Before Anne could shout at her, CC saw a black bear run around to the front of the car to the driver's side and pound on the window. Anne screamed.

CC made herself very tall and talked loudly. She reached in her jacket pocket and threw her power bar across the parking lot. The bear sniffed the air but it was not interested. The black bear charged CC. She reached into her pocket and felt for the small glass vial, struggling with the cap. She flung the ghost pepper powder at the black bear which had stopped feet in front of her, standing on its hind legs. The bear shook its head and sneezed. It shook its head again and sneezed again. It ran into the woods with one last glance at the girls as CC watched. She looked at the small empty vial and smiled. *It really does make everything better*, she thought. Getting back in the car, she asked Anne, "What were you thinking?" She grabbed the sandwich from Anne's hand and threw it out the window.

"What'd you do that for?" Anne protested. "He's gone now and I'm hungry."

CC started the engine and began the trek down toward Cherokee. "You know, Anne, the Great Smoky Mountain Park is the most visited national park in the United States. There are over nine million visitors each year. The Smoky Mountains gets its name from the blue fog or mist that hangs over the mountains and in the valleys. The Cherokee Indians settled it. They called it Shaconage or the place of blue smoke. The fog is a result of warm humid air from the Gulf of Mexico cooling rapidly as it enters higher elevations."

Anne looked down, wishing she had time to finish her ham sandwich while CC droned on. CC's monotone was making her tired. She fought to keep her eyes open. The sun was setting as Anne finally gave in and closed her eyes. A pounding rain began, hitting the top of the bus. What seemed like seconds later, CC shook her awake.

"Don't be alarmed, Anne, but the engine died. I can't pull over, the river is starting to pour over onto the road. I'm going to coast down as carefully as I can."

"What are you talking about?" Anne tried to shake herself awake.

The storm intensified. The VW bus wipers were swishing at high intensity but it wasn't enough to clear the windshield so CC could see. The VW rolled down out the exit of the Great Smoky Mountain Parkway. CC managed to maneuver it off the pavement to the gravel shoulder. It was pitch dark under the canopy of the old growth hickory trees. Anne quickly pushed the button down to lock her door and turned to CC. “What about the bears? We can’t get out of the car.”

CC tried her cell phone but there was no reception. “I’m sure someone will be by. There’s 60,000 people who visit here every day.” Lightning crashed through the distance, and thunder rolled across the mountain.

“But it’s dark; it’s rainy. You took my sandwich.” The lightning flashed again. Anne swore she saw a herd of bears standing on their hind legs, one of them holding her ham sandwich. “CC, do bears hunt at night? How about coyotes, wolves, mountain lions? What about snakes?”

“Anne, we’re fine. We’re fine inside this German-engineered piece of art.”

“You mean the piece of art that just broke down.” Anne lifted her finger to show the rain dripping off it. The flip-top sunroof was leaking and Anne was getting wet.

CC was noticeably annoyed. When it came to anything German, she took her heritage very seriously. After an hour without any cars passing by, a pair of headlights appeared driving around the bend in front of them, heading up the trail towards the mountains.

An old Jeep wrangler stopped just feet in front of the VW. Anne grabbed CC’s arm. “What do we do?”

“Let’s take a look at him and see. I’ll roll the window down a little.”

A very tall and muscular Native American man exited the old Jeep. Through the rain and the glow of the headlights, they could see he was wearing a beaded vest with multicolored feathers. He knocked on the window through the pouring rain.

CC rolled it down.

"Do you need help?" he asked in a deep voice.

Anne's eyes opened wide. She wanted to scream *Indian*! but knew how politically incorrect that was. She stifled back a giggle.

"Yes, I think I blew a gasket," CC said.

"The nearest tow truck is miles away. I can take you back to my village and have your car picked up. It's not safe to stay here at night."

CC looked at Anne who smiled. There was something about his eyes that were truthful. "My name is John Blackbear, Chief Blackbear."

He escorted Anne and CC through the pouring rain into his jeep and made a U-turn onto the road and headed up to the Oconaluftee Village. He talked while he drove. "The village is closed to visitors at this time of night but we can find you some accommodations. They might not be what you're used to. It's a little primitive. The village is a replica of an 18th century Cherokee community. It's to celebrate my ancestors who were allowed to stay here during the evacuation of the Trail of Tears."

CC broke in and explained, "You know, Anne, the Trail of Tears began in 1838 when the Cherokee land in the south was taken by the government and the Cherokee were forced west."

"My people, the Oconaluftee, received permission from the government to stay in North Carolina," John Blackbear said.

"That's right," CC said. "It was thanks to the efforts of William H. Thomas that they were able to stay here."

"You know your history," John Blackbear said.

"Thank you," CC said. She prided herself on knowing all manner of history.

They pulled up in front of the tribal council house, a large circular, windowless building situated on top of a mound. A stream ran next to it. The walls were made of saplings woven together and plastered with mud. Inside, there were animal skins on the floor and a roaring fire in the center with smoke rising up through the opening in the ceiling.

"We try to make the council house as authentic as possible," John Blackbear said. "Come sit by the fire and get warm. I'll get you some dry clothes."

A Cherokee woman returned carrying two dresses manufactured from a calico print with triangles and circles and the seven-sided star of the Cherokee. "My Cherokee name is Standing Deer but you can call me Sue. Here are some dry clothes." She was wearing a similar dress and Minnetonka moccasins.

"These are beautiful. Where can I buy one of these?" Anne held the dress up.

"We sell them in the gift shop. They are called tear dresses. They are the style of dress that our women wore during the Trail of Tears when they no longer had access to scissors because the government took them. The fabric was torn from larger pieces and then sewn together."

When she left, Anne and CC put on the dresses and laid out their wet clothes in front of the fire to dry. John Blackbear opened the deerskin that covered the entrance and walked in. "You look very good," he said, staring at Anne.

Anne did a slight curtsey and gave him a smile.

John Blackbear managed a smile back. "I've contacted a local mechanic who will pick up your car later. You are welcome to stay here. We have a guesthouse."

"Couldn't we just stay here tonight? The fire is so inviting," Anne said.

"That would be fine if you are comfortable. I've asked Sue to bring you some food. Please sit."

"Chief Blackbear, I've noticed you are wearing your ceremonial clothes," CC said, sitting cross-legged on the floor.

"Yes, we were reenacting the Nuwtiegwa, the festival of the October new moon. We had to stop because of the rain." He paused before explaining. "The Cherokee believe the earth was created at this time. This is when our new year begins." He handed Anne and CC each a crystal. "During this festival, each member of the tribe looks into the crystal to see if they will live through the next year. If they see themselves standing as they look into the stone, they will live. If they appear flat, they will die before the first spring moon."

"What did you see?" Anne asked.

"I saw that I met a very attractive maiden."

Anne looked at CC and then back at Chief Blackbear. He was still looking at her. She looked into her crystal and didn't see anything. Sue returned to the lodge, carrying bags from Taco Bell. "Is this part of the ceremonial food?" Anne asked giggling.

John Blackbear smiled again. As they sat cross-legged in front of the fire eating their ceremonial Chalupas, John Blackbear explained more about his people's culture. "My people believe that certain beings came down from on high and formed the world, the moon and the stars. It was believed that the world was created at the time of the new moon in autumn. The Cherokees believe that the morning star was once a wicked priest who killed people by witchcraft. When the Cherokee planned to kill him, he took all of his crystals and flew to the sky where he now appears as the morning star. Our tribe had the original morning star crystal. It was a natural seven-pointed quartz like our Cherokee emblem. It had been with our people for a thousand years. My people believed it had great power.

They used it during the October ceremony at morning's first light, which is the first day of the New Year. The chief would hold it up in the early morning light and it would shine like the morning star from the light of the sun. When it shined on the council house, it would make a perfect seven-pointed Cherokee star. This crystal was our greatest treasure." He gestured to their hands. "The crystals you hold are copies."

"Could we see the original morning star?" Anne asked.

"It was stolen many years ago. I do have a painting of it." They walked to the other side of the fire. On the wall was an early 1800s woodblock etching of a young Indian maiden holding a large seven-pointed crystal up toward the sun. "Look." John Blackbear pointed at the crystal. "You can see its imperfections here. Each crystal is unique. Their imperfections are like fingerprints. These are the original fingerprints of our people."

Anne peered at it closely. "I can see it. They are unique. May I take a picture?"

John nodded his permission. Anne took out her iPhone and zoomed in on the crystal. She snapped a few photos.

CC stifled a yawn. It had been a long drive filled with many adventures. As John Blackbear continued his stories, she lay down, covered herself with a deerskin blanket and fell asleep.

Anne sat cross-legged in front of John Blackbear, listening intently. She thought how handsome he was. She didn't really hear what he was saying but admired his many colorful feathers and his silver jewelry. She wondered if there were similar pieces in the gift shop. She would have to check on that in the morning.

"Anne," she heard. It broke her trance.

"Yes, John? I mean, Chief?"

"Anne, you can call me John. You look like you were falling asleep. Do you wish to lay down?"

"No, I want to hear more. It's fascinating."

"We don't want to wake your friend. The rain has stopped. My house is a short walk away. We can talk more there." He stood up and lowered his hand. Anne placed her hand in his. He had very strong hands. He nearly lifted her off the ground. Nigel had never been quite strong enough to lift her and his hands were long and bony and rather smooth, just the opposite of John Blackbear's.

They walked along a stone path that led from the council house past the gift shop and through a canopy of birch trees. Now that the rains had stopped, the sky was washed with stars and the moon highlighted the walk. John Blackbear walked next to Anne, nearly a foot taller than her. His sleeveless vest accented his muscles that rippled as his arms moved. She thought he couldn't be much older than her. Maybe in his forties. He was probably married but she hadn't noticed any wedding rings but then she thought do Cherokee wear wedding rings? She longed for cell service so she could Google it.

As they entered the clearing, she expected to see a teepee. Instead she saw a beautiful 6,000 square-foot, three-story log cabin with two giant oak trees for pillars. The double front door was eight feet wide and ten feet tall. Anne stopped in her tracks and looked up. "Ohmigod, what is this?"

"This is my home. You were expecting a teepee?"

Anne smiled. "Of course not. But. . ."

"We also operate a very large casino, very profitable." He opened the door for Anne. She walked into an entryway that soared up three stories. All the walls were hand-cut timber from the Smoky Mountains and carved with Indian totems. "These tell the story of my people," he said.

As they walked into the great room, there was a huge fieldstone fireplace that took up the entire length of the wall. John picked up a remote off a table, hit a button and the fire burst to life. "This is absolutely beautiful," Anne said.

"Come sit; I'll get us something to drink."

Anne sat on the long leather couch. She felt the fabric. It felt like the softest, buttery Coach leather purse. There were antiques, not just traditional Cherokee but Smoky Mountain mining and farming tools. There was also a Remington painting of wild stallions and one of an Indian scout. She got up to look at it closer and saw it was an original Remington. Before she could finish the last part of her "Holy. . ." John Blackbear returned wearing jeans and a flannel shirt. His dark thick black hair was tied back in a ponytail. He was carrying a bottle of wine and two glasses. He placed them on the tree trunk coffee table and opened the wine.

"You have a very good eye," Anne said. "I've seen Remingtons like that in the Museum of the West."

"My wife decorated the house. She is a collector of antiques and has a very good eye for such things. I built the house."

As he poured Anne a glass of wine, she downed it. Chief Blackbear answered the question she was dreading to ask. John filled his glass and sat down next to Anne. "The house was built by local craftsmen. The trees were harvested from felled trees. There are strict laws in the Smoky Mountains about harvesting timber. The land belongs to the Cherokee but we respect the mountains and only take what we need." He took a sip of his wine. "It took three years to build this house."

"We're not going to wake your wife, are we?" Anne asked.

"Not unless she can hear us from L.A."

"Is she on a trip?"

"No, she lives there with her new husband."

Anne sighed in relief.

"We were divorced two years ago."

Anne motioned with her empty glass. He filled it again. This time she sipped it. "I'm sorry to hear that."

"Don't be. It was a very amicable divorce. We're still friends." John Blackbear glanced at her bare left hand and asked, "How about you? I noticed you're not wearing a ring."

"Oh, no; I'm not married. I've never been married. I've devoted myself to my career."

"What do you do?"

"I'm an antique hunter." She paused. "I'm a chemist, too, but that's part time. I devote my life to antique hunting. In fact, that's what brought us to North Carolina. We're heading to Hickory. We've been commissioned to find musical antiques and vintage instruments for a client. We're heading to Nashville eventually but I wanted to stop at the antique mall in Hickory."

John held up his finger to motion *wait a minute* and walked out. When he returned, he was carrying a Gibson 1910 mandolin.

"That's beautiful." Anne held it up and studied it.

"It was a gift. I don't play. You can have it for your collection."

"I couldn't possibly. Do you know how much this is worth?"

"Please, I want you to have it."

Lost in her excitement, she leaned over and kissed John on the cheek. "Thank you so much!" She stopped and realized that she had kissed a complete stranger and looked shocked.

John pulled her in and kissed her on her lips.

Chapter Nine

CC rolled over and stretched. The fire had died down to embers. She felt the warmth of the morning sun as it cascaded through the smoke opening of the council house. She gave a big yawn. She had slept really well. She hoped Anne had been able to sleep also. She looked over and Anne was not there.

She stood up, stretched her legs. She changed into her dry clothes and walked out of the council house. It was a rather warm October morning but still she could smell winter coming. The sun warmed her skin. She looked around and saw the costume adorned Cherokee preparing for a day full of tourists. She recognized Sue and walked over. "Good morning, Sue. Have you seen my friend, Anne?"

"I have not seen her since last night."

CC went into the small coffee shop, adjacent to the village. She sat down at the counter and ordered a cup of coffee. She finished it and spun around on the stool in time to see Anne walking up the path of birches. She was still wearing her tear dress. CC ran out to greet her. Anne's hair was disheveled. She was wearing a colorful feather in her hair and a smile. "Anne, where have you been? I was worried sick."

"So worried that you couldn't wait to have breakfast with me?"

"I needed some caffeine so I could go search for you. You're up early?"

The smile Anne was wearing grew wider.

"Why are you smiling?"

"I had a very nice night."

"I slept well, too."

"I didn't sleep."

"What are you talking about? Why do you have a feather in your hair?"

Anne reached up and pulled the feather out. She had forgotten that John Blackbear had put it there. "We should get going if we're going to make Hickory. The van's been fixed and paid for."

"What do you mean paid for?"

"John took care of it."

They walked to the parking lot where the VW was waiting. They climbed in and headed back down the mountain and to Hickory.

As CC drove, Anne pulled out her iPhone and looked at the photos she'd taken of the morning star crystal. "I'd really like to find this for John."

"What are you talking about?"

"I think you were asleep by then but John was telling me about his tribe's crystal. It was used in the October New Year ceremony. It was stolen a long time ago."

"When we stop tonight," said CC, "I'm going to blog about the reservation and everything that happened. You can mention the crystal and we can upload the pictures."

"That's a great idea, CC; we can also post pictures of the mandolin."

"Mandolin?"

Anne reached into the back and pulled up the case. She opened it and showed CC the 1910 Gibson sunburst mandolin. "Isn't it beautiful?"

CC took a sideways glance. "Where'd you find that?"

"It was in the village."

"How much was it?"

"Very reasonable. Betsy will be pleased."

"When we get to the antique mall, let's remember our priority is to find pieces for Betsy. If we come across other items for fans on our list that we can buy, that's fine. The priority is Betsy, right?"

Anne stared at the picture of the morning star crystal. She thought about John and then she thought about Nigel. *What was she going to tell Nigel?* It wasn't that they were exclusive or that they were even serious, but she should have told Nigel about her feelings before she left. She'd left him hanging like she had for the past year. He was such a sweet man she didn't want to hurt him. She would have to call him later.

Chapter Ten

Anne was a little disappointed at the exterior of the Hickory Antiques Mall. It wasn't quaint, it wasn't charming; it looked like an abandoned K-Mart without a soul. It was a big glass storefront building with poorly painted white aluminum and a big ugly sign that read Hickory Antiques Mall.

"This place had good reviews on *Yelp*. Let's get past the façade of the building." Anne pulled out her notebook that contained all the requests from their fans. It was color coded according to style and era and price. Since the *Chicago Tribune* article heralded them as heroes for solving the "Estate Sale Murders," the Spoon Sisters' blog had reached more than 50,000 fans—some from as far away as Europe and the Middle East.

Anne followed CC into the shop. Amidst the turn of the century dressers, there was an original Globe Wernicke 1930s barrister bookcase. Anne looked at the four-stack mahogany case. The wood had been restored to its original finish. At $575, it was an average price, but she knew CC would not make room for it in the bus. In the corner next to the bookcase, was an old green glass stand-up ashtray. Its base was cast metal. A brass dragon swooped over the jadeite bowl. She inspected it, and it appeared to be an art deco original. She checked her list; Clyde from Romeoville was looking for an antique ashtray for his man cave. She snapped a picture and texted it to him.

CC came over to look. She was holding a Sunbeam wooden basket that had been used to deliver bread in the 1930s. "Anne, I think I'm going to get this for my photo supplies," she said. "I have something else to show you."

CC grabbed Anne and pulled her over to a small table in the corner where a very large man sat on a very small wooden stool. In front of him, there were several cigarette cards that resembled modern day baseball cards. There was also other tobacco memorabilia including cigarette lighters, tobacco tins, cigar boxes and ashtrays.

The man looked like Burl Ives except a little less friendly. "Anne, do you see what I see?" CC pointed. The cigarette cards on display depicted Native Americans. One card had a picture of John L. Sullivan, the famous heavyweight champion boxer. But the one that got CC's heart pumping was the 1887 Allen & Ginter card of Adrian Cap Anson, a famous baseball player in the 1880s. It was an N28, the rarest available. It depicted the Chicago White Stockings/Colts player in his uniform, bat in hand. Even though the card was far from perfect, it was almost impossible to find. All the cards on the table ranged from the late 1880s to the 1930s.

Mr. Ives smiled when he saw CC recognize the Cap Anson card.

CC knew that he knew that she knew what it was worth. All the cards were enclosed in protective sleeves. "May I take a closer look at the Cap?"

"Honey, please, go right ahead. Be gentle." He kept a watchful eye on her as she slid it out of its protective covering.

CC turned it over gently in her hands. "It's remarkable. How did you come across all these cards?"

"They're on consignment from one of my long-time customers and friend, Randall Bement."

CC replaced the card and did a mental inventory. She estimated what she thought she could pay compared to what she could sell them for. Then she remembered someone on her list who collected tobacco memorabilia. The whole collection would be perfect for him. 'Excuse us for a moment." She pulled Anne to the corner by the Coke machine.

She pulled out her iPhone 6 plus and texted Dr. Sherwin, a pulmonologist from Massachusetts who collected smoking memorabilia. "Anne, these cards would be remarkable for his office. He could frame them and display them." She texted the pictures that she had taken of the cards and sent them to Dr. Sherwin.

Anne's phone vibrated. Clyde had responded that he wanted the ashtray but for no more than $150. Perhaps they could strike a deal if CC bought the tobacco memorabilia. Dr. Sherwin texted CC back with the message, "Buy at any price."

CC and Anne walked back towards Mr. Ives, smiling. The song "Silver and Gold" played through CC's head. She tried to shake the tune but couldn't. "I'm CC Muller, by the way; this is my friend, Anne Hillstrom."

CC waited to hear him give the name *Burl Ives* but instead, he said, "Earl."

"So, Earl, do you have a price for the whole collection?"

He sat back on the small stool. It balanced on its back two tiny wooden legs. Under his great girth, they seemed more like toothpicks than legs. They creaked a warning. "I've never thought about selling everything all at once. I always believed I'd make more selling them piecemeal. If I had to put a number on it, I would say that the Cap card alone is worth at least $1,200 and I'd throw in the rest for $4,500."

CC knew that Dr. Sherwin would be happy at $6,000. He was one of the wealthiest physicians on the east coast. It was less about getting a bargain and more about acquiring what he wanted. "At $4,000 we could have a deal."

"Wait," Anne interrupted. "There's one more thing. Could you do $100 on that standing ashtray near the bookcase?"

Earl leaned further back, now balancing on one toothpick. CC desperately wanted him to speak before the stool collapsed. "I believe at $4,200 we have a deal for the cards and the ashtray. How could I say no to two such lovely ladies as yourselves?"

CC reached over the table and shook his hand. "Does Mr. Bement have more cards or more tobacco antiques?"

Earl smiled. "His whole house is full of stuff. He's a picker."

"Is he coming in? May I leave my card?" CC handed him one of the Spoon Sisters' cards.

"Randall hasn't been in for a couple weeks. It's hard for him to get around."

"Would it be possible to stop by his house?"

"Let me give him a call." With a great effort, Earl heaved himself off the stool, which creaked a sigh of relief, and wobbled over to a rotary dial phone. After a brief conversation, he came back to the girls, handed them a piece of paper with Randall's address. "I told Randall that you purchased his whole table. He's very pleased. He said he'd be willing to see you today but only if you go now."

Anne didn't wait. She headed for the door, holding the heavy ashtray stand. "Thank you, Earl," CC said as she followed Anne out.

Chapter Eleven

Randall Bement's house was a few blocks off of Main Street. It was a simple, unassuming one-story home. A wooden ramp had been built over the stairs leading to the front door. The front door was open; the screen door wasn't. CC knocked and called inside. "Randall, it's CC. Earl sent us!" Anne peeked over her shoulder, anxious to take a look around inside.

They could hear the hum of the motorized wheelchair as Randall made his way around the piles of junk that cluttered the living room. Randall arrived at the door wearing his oxygen cannula and his NASCAR baseball cap. Unlike his friend Earl, Randall was very slight in stature. He smiled a yellow grin and unlatched the screen door.

Years of smoking, CC thought. "Ladies, come in please." Randall put the chair in reverse to make room for Anne and CC. He seemed to know his way around the slalom without having to look. "Earl told me you bought my whole table. That's wonderful. You got some really good pieces."

"I know. We were excited to find them and we're hoping you might have more."

"Take a look around. I've been picking for 50 years."

CC glanced around the crowded room and saw stacks of tobacco tins, old advertising leaflets and cigar cutters. "I take it you collect tobacco-related items?"

"My family's been in the tobacco business since before the war," Randall replied.

"Which war was that?" Anne asked as she eyed a marble-topped antebellum cherry wood side table. In her head, she calculated the dimensions to see if it would fit in the VW and her already cluttered living room.

"Honey, you're in the south; there's only one war," Randall said.

Then she eyed the 16-inch tall table globe that was encased in rosewood. Its fittings were brass. She walked over to it and spun it around. "Is this from the war?"

"It was at my family's tobacco plantation. My ancestor brought it over from England. It's a rare globe. The capitals are real rubies."

"It's beautiful." Anne ran her hand over it. "Would you be willing to sell it?" Anne thought about Mr. Gunter, the business executive and philanthropist, who was always looking for unique pieces for his collection. He displayed these pieces at his museum located inside the turn-of-the-century house he had restored in downtown Chicago. This would be perfect for the smoking room. Then she laughed out loud and thought, *Smoking*! How appropriate.

"I'm not ready to part with it yet." Randall shook his head. "I only sold the tobacco cards because I needed money for George."

"George?" CC asked.

Randall did a 180 in the chair and waved for the girls to follow him. He went into the kitchen where a big orange tabby lay on the checkerboard linoleum under the hickory table. "This is George. He hasn't been feeling too well."

Anne bent down to pet the tabby. His eyes opened a bit and then closed. Cats normally purred when Anne was around; this was unusual. "Poor dear. You're not feeling so well, are you?" Anne noticed his whiskers were crusty as though he had been throwing up. "Has George gotten into something outside in the back yard? Some plants?"

"George never goes out. He's strictly a house cat. I've been feeding him the same food for ten years. He's been real tired and threw up a couple times."

Spotting more cigarette cards on the table, CC said, "Do you mind if I look at those?" At his nod, she sat down and leafed through them.

Anne walked around the kitchen. "Has George been to the vet?"

"When he first started throwing up, I brought him to the clinic. They did some tests. They didn't find anything wrong. They said to make sure he drank water and watch him."

Anne walked over to the kitchen back door, which opened to the large backyard. The old wooden door had a beautiful leaded-glass window that encompassed more than half of it. "This door is beautiful."

"I brought that from the plantation, too. That's got to be early 1800s. It took a lot of work to fit it."

Anne stared out through the glass. The afternoon sun was breaching the roof of the house, the shadows in the yard were running away as the first ray of light struck the cut glass. She had to cover her eyes from the glare. "It's like a magnifying glass. That's really bright."

Behind her was a walk-in pantry which was completely dark except for the beam of light coming through the door. *It was like a beacon,* Anne thought, so she followed it. At the back of the dark pantry, behind boxes of oatmeal and grits, was a wooden bin. That's when Anne figured out what George's problem was. Above the potato bin, the bags of brown sugar were trickling down onto the potatoes. The light from the afternoon sun focused on the potatoes and had turned them green from the chlorophyll.

Anne walked out of the pantry, holding a green potato that had been nibbled at. "Randall, I think I found what's been bothering George. That little beam coming through the kitchen door turns the potatoes green. That green on the potato is caused by chlorophyll which is not toxic, but the light exposure also increased the production of an alkaloid called solanine." She paused and put the potato down on the table. "The more intense the light, the more solanine is produced. That door window acts like a magnifying glass and strengthens the beam. Consuming solanine can make you pretty sick. The highest concentration is in the skin of the potato. These potatoes have a high concentration. Normally, they would taste bitter and George would take one nibble and walk away, but some brown sugar dusted them, making them taste sweet."

"My dear George." Randall rolled over to George. "I forgot those potatoes were even in there. I can't get that far back into the pantry in this wheelchair. What do I do?" he turned to Anne.

"It doesn't look like George ingested a lot. I think the best thing is to continue to watch him. Give him some high protein Lysine." She pulled a foil-wrapped package out of her large orange Prada bag. "This will help his immune system. CC and I will clean up the potatoes for you so George doesn't get tempted again."

"How can I ever thank you?" Randall asked. Anne could see his eyes tearing up. She could tell how much George meant to him. She understood because she felt the same about her white Persian, Sassy. She would be devastated if anything happened to her. When they had finished cleaning the pantry, Randall offered them some ice tea. They sat at the kitchen table. "Anything you want, just take," he said.

"I couldn't do that," CC said. "I want to give you a fair price. I have someone who would love these tobacco cards."

Anne looked over his shoulder at the marble side table. It would fit in her living room if she moved a few things. It wouldn't fit in the bus. That's when she saw the blue uniform on a chair in the corner. Walking over the piles that made her feel at home, she held up the pristine navy wool coat with gold buttons.

"That belonged to my four times grandfather," Randall said. "He was a federal soldier. Are you interested in military memorabilia? I have some of his swords. Most of his possessions are promised to the Lenoir-Rhyne University collection. I have many of his letters also. He was a very eloquent man. He kept a journal during the 1838 evacuation."

Anne stopped, staring at the uniform. "Evacuation?"

"The Cherokee removal project as it was known."

Anne took a breath. "May I see it?"

He rolled over to the small bookcase in the living room and handed Anne a worn, leather-bound brown book. Its pages were yellowed and the writing faded. Inside was a daguerreotype of young Private Randall Bement standing next to a Cherokee Indian.

Anne read out loud, "This is my account of what happened. I was born in Catawba County, North Carolina, the only son to Jebediah Bement, a tobacco farmer outside of Hickory. As a boy, I hunted and fished these lands. I grew up alongside many Cherokee. They taught me to hunt the wild boar and timber wolves and to speak their language." She paused and looked at Randall. "This is incredible. I'd love to read this." She thought for a moment. "Is there anyway I could take it with me, make copies and send it back?"

Randall sat back in his chair and thought for a minute. "You know what, hon, I have a copy right here.

I promised the actual journal to the historical society but I made a copy." He reached into a kitchen drawer and pulled out a stack of papers. They appeared to be photocopies of the journal held together with a binder clip. He handed it to her.

Anne could make out the scribbled handwriting. It was faint but still legible. "Thank you. This is wonderful."

Behind her, CC coughed and nodded at her watch. "Randall, thanks so much for letting us stop by and sharing your history with us," Anne said. "We have to get going."

Randall watched them leave. Anne and CC loaded their purchases into the VW bus. "If we buy much more, we're going to need to rent a U-Haul," CC said as she started the ignition.

Anne was not opposed to the idea. She pulled out her smart phone and Googled U-Haul trucks. When CC gave her a look, she put her phone down and pulled out the copy of the journal. "Hey, CC, some of these pages are a little easier to read than others. Listen to this: When I was hunting one year, I found a young Cherokee squaw. She had been shot by hunters and left for dead. I tended her wound and carried her to the spring. When she was able to continue, I took her to my hunting lodge and cared for her until she was strong enough. I learned her name was Immookalee, which means *waterfall* in English. We became friends and she taught me her language.

"When she had recovered enough to travel, I took her to her people. Her father was the great chief and was grateful to me. He let me stay in the village." The papers flew out of Anne's hand scattering across the floorboards as CC slammed on the brakes to avoid missing a gas tanker who was swerving around a slow moving car.

"Watch it, CC," Anne said. "Now I've lost my place." While Anne was picking up the scattered pages of the journal, her text message alert sounded. She reached into her large orange Prada bag and pulled out her phone. The text was from Nigel.

"Who is it, Anne?" CC asked.

"It's Nigel. I forgot to tell him that I was going out of town. He wants to go to the movies tonight."

"Anne, really? Isn't it time you told Nigel how you really feel? You're not being fair to him, are you?"

"CC, I don't know what to say. I enjoy his company. I like going out with him but he doesn't make me feel like . . ." She stopped, realizing she hadn't explained to CC what had happened last night at the reservation.

"Feel like what, Anne?"

"You know. Exciting. Tingly."

CC wanted to end the conversation right there.

"I'll text him."

"Anne, you can't do that. You owe it to him to tell him in person."

"All right." Anne texted back. "I'd love to go to the show but I'm on my way to Nashville. Wish you were here," she read aloud as she typed. "There. See."

CC swerved slightly on the highway. "Watch out," Anne said.

"I was looking at the mountains. Anne, they're so beautiful," CC said, pointing to the tall mountain looming in front of them. The smoke billowed at the top creating a blue fog. "You know, Anne, the Smoky Mountains were the first national park in the entire system."

"That's great, CC." Anne clutched the armrest, hanging on for dear life as trucks flew by, going around zigzag turns with enough *g* force to lift their tires off the ground. CC seemed unconcerned about the rain that had started. She kept looking right and left at the view rather than at the road.

"You know, Anne, the Smoky Mountain range is the heaviest forested range in the world. And there are two black bears for every square mile."

"We've already had our quota of black bears. Watch the road," Anne said. The VW bus hydroplaned over the pavement, gliding. Anne was truly terrified now. She had gone from mildly upset to downright nauseous. "CC, don't you think you should slow down?"

"Anne, this old bus was built for the Autobahn." A Dually F250 with rebel flags in the rear window and more rebels in the bed flew by, one of them waving at CC who smiled back at the young shirtless farm boys. The gentle rain gave way to a blue rainbow as the sun broke through the fog on the mountains. Anne saw a billboard that read *Tobacco Barn, area's largest antique store, 70,000 square feet with over 70 dealers.*

Anne's nerves settled. Finally, a calm in the storm. "CC, did you see the billboard?"

"Yes, Anne. I'm going to pull off at the Asheville exit. We have to stop."

Chapter Twelve

They drove down the exit ramp onto the two-lane street that bordered the river and led into Asheville. They pulled up to the Tobacco Barn, an old warehouse that was once used as a tobacco factory. In a Mercedes springer van next to them, a road-weary family from Florida piled out. Three screaming blond-haired children jumped out first, followed by a haggard mother. Anne popped some Tylenol. The father ignored the children, motioning to a young Spanish nanny to corral them and keep them quiet. Anne popped a few more Tylenol. Between the children and CC's driving, her nerves had reached a critical state.

Outside of the large steel delivery doors were hundreds of wrought iron gates, some as small as three feet, others 20 feet wide by eight feet tall. CC stopped to gaze longingly at them, picturing them in her garden.

"I'm going inside," Anne said, walking through the large overhead door. She was greeted by the smell of tobacco and must. She marveled at the expanse of the warehouse. The first thing Anne came across was a table piled high with hurricane lanterns—some iron, some brass. Surrounding them was a mishmash of garden art and cement lawn statutes. Every aisle was packed full with antiques and salvaged sconces, stained glass windows, leaded-glass doors and lots and lots of furniture.

Anne walked up to a long table with linen. The sign read "lace linen." The handwritten tag on a tablecloth read "$300, 1920s hand-sewn Irish lace."

A young couple next to Anne was looking at an ivory tablecloth embroidered with red and green leaves. Anne could tell immediately that it wasn't old. She overheard the young woman say it would be perfect for their new home. Apparently, they had just gotten married. "Excuse me," Anne said. "Are you going to buy that tablecloth?"

The young woman was wearing a short orange dress and high, matching, orange wedge heels. Her face beamed. "Yes, it's absolutely beautiful. My parents gave us a dining room set for a wedding present and this would be perfect on it."

"You know it's not authentic, right?" Anne said.

"No, I didn't."

"Smell it. What does it smell like?"

The young woman held the linen up to her nose and took a deep whiff. "It smells like tea."

"Yes, sometimes dealers take a new linen that resembles the original and they soak it in tea to give it an aged patina," Anne explained.

The girl smelled it again. "I didn't notice it. The whole building smells like tobacco. I never would have thought of sniffing it."

"It's a good rule of thumb if you're looking at antique linens."

"Do you work here?" the girl asked, setting the tablecloth back on the table.

"Oh, no." Anne retrieved her card from the bottom of her purse. "I'm an antique hunter. We can help you find whatever you need."

The young woman looked at her new husband and then back at Anne. "Ma'am."

"You can call me, Anne."

"Would you mind helping us look around?"

"Not at all; it would be fun."

Before they could move to the next booth, a middle-aged woman tapped on Anne's shoulder. "I'm so sorry. I overheard your whole explanation to her. I was wondering if you would mind looking at this vase. It's marked *Chinese* and priced $500. Can you tell me if this is authentic? It says it's over 300 years old."

Anne picked up the 23-inch colorful vase decorated with dogwood branches. She held it up to her mouth and licked it. The woman stared in shock. "I'm checking the temperature of it to see if there's been any restoration done," Anne said.

The woman didn't know how to respond and watched fascinated. When Anne was done, she handed the vase back to the woman. "Some of the vase is authentic; some is not."

"What do you mean?" The woman gave her a quizzical look.

"Sometimes a dealer has an authentic antique. They break it into pieces and incorporate those pieces and make several replicas from the original antique. It's almost impossible to see where it was glued together. The difference in the thickness of the material will transfer heat differently. That's how I can tell it's been restored."

"Thank you so much. Do you mind if I tag along?" Anne led the couple and the woman throughout the store. When they reached the fine china there was an older couple, who were both wearing leather motorcycle vests. Anne thought they were cute; she had seen their three-wheeler out in front. The biker granny chick was holding a porcelain dinner plate. The young couple said to the granny, "You should have Anne look at that for you."

The granny biker chick smiled at Anne and handed her the plate. Anne pulled out a small penlight. She held the plate up over her head and shined the light through it. "Fine porcelain should be translucent. You can see where this plate has been restored. Where the light doesn't shine through is where they fixed the crack."

CC finished looking at the iron gates. She walked into the tobacco barn. In the center of the aisle, she saw a crowd of people zig-zagging up and down like a dragon float at a Chinese New Year parade. CC asked the young girl at the register, "What's going on down there?"

The girl shrugged.

By the time CC reached the end of the warehouse, she saw Anne climb onto the top of a soapbox. "I'd be glad to help everyone but you have to wait your turn. Maybe we could do the larger items first. Who's here for the stained glass windows?" Several people raised their hands. "Who's here for furniture? There's a lovely Renaissance Belgian server with some lovely stained glass. It's a real bargain." Anne thought. She should know she coveted it herself.

CC made her way through the crowd and stood in front of Anne who was handing out business cards. "What are you doing?" She grabbed her arm and pulled her off her soapbox.

"CC, this is a real opportunity. I've handed out forty cards. I've already had people ask for help."

"Anne, I appreciate you trying to promote us. I just don't know how we're going to take on this extra work. Our focus has to be on Betsy."

"I found a bluegrass poster. It looks like a tent revival with some famous artists. I think it would be nice for Betsy's wall," Anne said. "Let me show you where it is." Anne walked through the crowd like she was Joan of Arc. She felt lifted. People touched her as she walked by. She felt like blessing them as she walked, but it was a faded fantasy.

"Here it is, CC—the poster I was telling you about." Anne stopped at a small booth which had crates full of record albums, 8 x 10 black and white photographs, some signed.

CC thumbed through the albums and admired the posters. She walked over to the small glass curio cabinet. Inside it was a 12-inch four-song EP self-titled Dave Southwell. "Anne, look at this!" CC said, pointing to the album behind the glass.

"I've never seen that album before. I have all Dave's CDs," Anne said. "Let's look at it." She flagged down the girl from the cash register who opened the case.

"They're asking $500. The price went up recently," the girl said.

Anne and CC gave each other knowing looks.

The register girl flipped it over to reveal Dave Southwell's signature. "This was a promotional EP that Dave put out before he was signed. It was never released. Real old school, recording on vinyl. I like that."

"May I take a look?" CC asked.

The girl handed it over to CC.

CC read the back cover. It said "Recorded at West End Studios, Nashville. Sound engineer: L. Walters." CC looked at Anne. "I think Betsy would love to have this." She turned back to the girl and they negotiated a price.

Chapter Thirteen

By the time they reached Gatlinburg, the only hotel they could find with a room was up in the mountains. The room suddenly became available, CC learned, after a tourist went a little too fast and fell off the side of the mountain. At least that's what the girl on the phone told her.

As they wound up the mountain, CC could see how you could easily fall off—there were no guardrails, and it was pouring rain again. Luckily, Anne was asleep. The little 120 horsepower VW bus chugged its way up the steep incline. CC saw the small sign pointing to Buckberry Lodge. She pulled in the parking lot which had enough room for ten cars, all of them luxury SUVS. Buckberry was a four-diamond resort literally hanging off the side of one of the area's largest mountains.

While CC checked in, Anne looked around. She thumbed through the books, including one about Popcorn Sutter, the original Hillbilly moonshiner. The small lobby was decorated with Smoky Mountain history, including photos and a stuffed coyote. Anne held up one of the little sleigh bells for sale with a tag warning, Ring if a bear approaches. "Does this work?" she asked the 19-year-old high school girl at the registration desk.

The girl smiled and said, "No."

They got a room and parked in front of the lodge. All the rooms were suites in a log cabin style. CC opened the door to their room. It had a bearskin rug, a fireplace and an oversized rocking chair. She opened

French doors to a small wood balcony. It had two Adirondack chairs. Even though it was dark, she could still see what she thought was a bear a couple hundred feet down in the gulley among the tall trees. "Anne, come out and take a look!" she called into the room.

Anne walked out, reading the signed Popcorn Sutter book she had bought. "This is beautiful." She gazed out over the railing.

The moon was waning, lighting up the mountains and the woods in front. They sat in the chairs and stared out. It was getting late, and they needed to hurry to make it to the top of the lodge where the gourmet restaurant was. CC walked up the path to the restaurant, with Anne trudging behind, watching over her shoulder for bears. While they waited to be seated, they sat in overstuffed leather chairs in front of a stone fireplace that was blazing. The steward brought them both a glass of local blackberry wine. CC sipped. "This is very good."

It was a mild evening, allowing guests to sit outside on the wraparound porch that overlooked the mountains. Anne and CC ate at a small table in a corner with a magnificent view of the Smoky Mountains, lit up by moonlight. CC had shrimp with a potato, bacon and onion gratin. Anne had filet sliders with a remoulade sauce. For dessert, they shared a warm chocolate cake with vanilla ice cream.

In the morning, after a good night's rest, Anne and CC headed back to the reception desk to check out and to enjoy the complimentary breakfast. "It will probably be yogurt and muffins. We can grab some for the road," CC said.

They were surprised to find a full breakfast including scrambled eggs, pecan bacon, corned beef hash, eggs benedict, pancakes, and fresh-squeezed orange juice. The hot biscuits were brought out with corn muffins. They sat on the deck overlooking the mountains. Two eagles flew overhead, dancing and twirling and dive-bombing into the gulley. Anne couldn't be more pleased as she slathered butter on her biscuit. She followed the butter with fresh raspberry jam from a local artisan. The taste was sweet. Anne looked up. "CC, I could live here."

As they ate, CC pulled out the Dave Southwell EP from her bag. On the front was a close-up of Dave sitting on a stool with his acoustic guitar in front of an old RCA microphone. It made sense to her now why Steven had wanted them to find the Johnny Cash microphone for Dave Southwell. The one on the cover was the same make and year. Dave looked young and full of hope in the photo. On the back cover were black and white photos from the session, the engineer's room, and the recording studio. Some people sat on a couch watching the recording. The last photo was from the engineer's point of view, looking over the recording console. "Anne, Dave looks like a kid here. He can't be more than seventeen or eighteen in this photo."

Anne licked the butter off the corner of her lip and took the EP from CC. "He was handsome back then, wasn't he?"

CC agreed silently with Anne. She picked up her coffee cup and stared out at the mountains.

Chapter Fourteen

By the time they arrived in Nashville, it was early evening. They pulled up at the Hermitage Hotel, a five-diamond luxury hotel built in the Beaux Arts era. Usually out of their price range, CC had been able to get a good deal due to her media rate.

As they pulled up, the concierge ran to open their doors. He held an umbrella over their heads even though there was just a gentle mist. He smiled a warm smile. He was an older gentleman but very distinguished looking. CC was reminded of Cary Grant. "Ladies, welcome to the Hermitage. My name is Bradley. I'm here at your service. I'll make sure your bags are brought up to your room." He escorted Anne and CC up the stairs into the lobby as the valet drove off in the VW.

Anne was struck by the magnificence of the lobby. Large brass planters with tall palms anchored the Italian marble columns. Comfortable couches and chairs sat underneath the painted glass skylight that easily spanned one hundred feet. Above the handcrafted fireplace hung a gilded French Renaissance mirror. A genuine Persian rug covered the floor underneath the sitting room. Anne coveted it. She thought even Jay Gatsby would be astounded by the opulence.

They checked into their room, which was as elegant as the lobby. It boasted two queen beds, a couch, a chair, and a writing desk. The private bathroom featured more marble, a large soaking tub, double vanities and a TV above the mirror. Anne was in heaven.

She sat down on the couch and watched CC who was unpacking. "Where do we start first? All the antique shops are closed," Anne said.

"Why don't we take the night off? There are a hundred bars up and down Broadway," CC said. "I thought we could go hear some music."

Anne grabbed her suitcase and ran into the bathroom. When she came out, she was wearing a knee-length skirt trimmed in fringe and brown cowboy boots.

"Where'd you get that?"

"I bought it in Gatlinburg when I ran into the boot shop." She spun around and the fringe spun around with her. "We're going line dancing, and I have to look the part."

"No cowgirl hat?" CC asked.

"Don't be ridiculous. I'm not going to mess my hair."

They walked the few blocks to Broadway, which was lined up and down with bars, honky tonks, souvenir shops and boot stores. The sounds of country music spilled out onto the sidewalk. They arrived at the Wild Horse Saloon for its nightly country line-dancing lesson. Anne dumped her large orange Prada bag on the table and ran onto the dance floor. CC sat and watched.

The dances started with the simple electric slide. Anne quickly picked up the steps, smiling and waving at CC. She tried to get her on the floor. It was a bit too hokey for CC. After a couple songs, Anne plopped down on the stool next to her. Sipping on an amaretto stone sour, Anne said, "Mmm, this is good. Aren't you going to try and dance, CC? It's so much fun."

"I'm fine just watching." CC sipped on her diet Coke. Anne took off for the dance floor again.

A man walked up to CC, his blonde hair pulled back in a topknot. His Gibson vintage guitar t-shirt was tight showing his muscular build. His jeans were tattered, a pair of brown snakeskin cowboy boots peeked out from the worn hem. CC knew he couldn't be any older than his late twenties. He looked barely legal. CC had noticed him when they first walked into the Wild Horse. He'd been talking to the bouncer. She caught a glance of his sea green eyes. "Can I buy you a drink?" he asked her.

"No, I'm just waiting for my friend. She's on the dance floor."

"How about we dance, then let me buy you a drink?"

The live band was loud. CC had to scream to be heard. "No, thank you, I don't dance."

"I can teach you. I'm a really good teacher."

CC looked over at Anne on the dance floor. Her arms were swinging wildly as she spun around. She could tell she was going to be a while. *Why not?* she thought.

"My name's Brent," he said, reaching down a hand to help her off the barstool.

"CC," she returned, putting her hand in his. They walked onto the dance floor.

"This is pretty simple." He pulled her in his arms. "Two steps forward and one step back. Follow my lead."

Meanwhile, Anne took a break from the dance floor to check her phone for messages. There were three from Nigel. "Where are you?" they asked. She texted him back. "In Nashville. I'm line dancing at the Wild Horse." She hit send, finished her drink and ran back to the dance floor. She joined CC and Brent as they did the electric slide and other line dances. CC's two left feet were stumbling into both Brent and Anne. "Stop it," Anne told her.

Brent just smiled.

After several drinks, Anne was getting tired, and CC was ready to go. "One last dance. I love this song. Then I promise we'll go," Anne said. She headed back to the floor and stood in line with the other dancers. She felt a tap on her shoulder. When she turned around, she saw a very tall and very British Nigel Towers, wearing jeans, cowboy boots, a black Stetson, a turquoise bolo tie and a gingham cotton shirt. Anne, feeling the effects of several drinks, was surprised but happy. "Nigel! What are you doing here?" She reached up, pulling him down by the bolo strings, giving him a big lingering kiss.

Nigel smiled back. "You told me to come."

Anne looked surprised. "What do you mean?"

"Your text message yesterday said you wished I was here."

Anne laughed. "It's just an expression that people say when they're having a good time. I didn't mean it literally."

Nigel's face turned red.

"Never mind. I'm glad you're here. Let's dance. I'll teach you."

"No need." Nigel knew every move from years of dance lessons when he was kid. His long spindly legs hopped around the floor like an elegant grasshopper. Anne couldn't stop smiling. He was so charming.

CC sat on the bar stool next to Brent. "That was fun. You're right; you're a good teacher." She leaned in closer to him.

When the song was over, Nigel and Anne came back over to their table.

Nigel tipped his hat to CC. "Howdy, ma'am,' he said in his best John Wayne imitation.

CC giggled. "What are you doing here?"

Anne grabbed CC's arm. "It's a long story. Doesn't he look great?" Anne slipped off the stool and landed on the floor laughing. CC and Nigel picked her up and set her back on the stool.

"Anne, I think we should get you back to the hotel."

"Don't be silly. The night just started," she said, slurring her words.

"Let me call us a cab," Nigel said.

"We can walk back. Anne needs some fresh air."

"I'll walk you back," said Nigel.

"It was really nice to meet you but as you can see I have to take my friend home," CC said to Brent.

"I'm playing at the Bluebird on Monday. Come see me, I'll leave your name at the door."

"I will if we're still in town." CC smiled.

"All right, then." Brent said, walking away.

"I need a breath mint." Anne reached into her large orange Prada bag and felt something silky between her fingers. She pulled out John Blackbear's feather and stared at it. She looked at Nigel. "We're fine. You don't have to walk with us," she said in a brusque voice.

Anne and CC walked out into the street onto Broadway. The neon lights on the cowboy boots twinkled over their heads. The music followed them out, fighting with the music coming from the other bars. Anne felt dizzy from all the stimulation.

"Are you okay, Anne?" CC asked, holding her up by the arm.

"I'll be fine. Let's get back to the hotel. I need to lie down."

They turned onto Third Avenue. "Look, here's a shortcut," CC said, leading Anne down the dark alley. The rain started up again, pouring on them. They ran along the uneven pavement, avoiding puddles. The rain poured downhill onto the street below. They stopped for a moment under a fire escape to let the rain let up. Anne pulled out the two rain ponchos she had bought earlier at Boot Barn. Anne had tried on a pair of $1,000

Tony Lama boots to see if they felt any different than her $250 pair. There was no difference. She wound up buying the $4 ponchos instead to combat the on and off rain.

Anne was crying.

"What's wrong? You don't feel well?" CC asked.

"No, it's Nigel. Did you see that big goof in his cowboy hat and boots? He looked like Woody from Toy Story. He's adorable. I have to let him go."

Lightning flashed, illuminating the alleyway. That's when CC saw someone standing in the shadows. She couldn't make out his face. CC put her hand out in front of Anne and pulled her back. "What are you doing?" Anne asked as her back hit the brick wall.

"Quiet," CC said. When the lightning flashed again, the man lunged at CC, brandishing a knife. She narrowly escaped the seven-inch blade.

Anne swung her large orange Prada bag at the man knocking the knife out of his hand. CC followed with a quick knee to the groin. The man doubled over. Anne delivered a final blow with her large orange Prada bag that held the brass art deco planter she'd bought earlier. The man in the alley landed facedown in a puddle of rainwater and blood. When the lightning flashed again, CC could see the blood dripping from his head wound down his tattooed neck. His hand twitched and he reached out trying to grab CC's leg.

"Run!" CC yelled as they darted past the man, through the alley and back onto the crowded street. By the time they reached the Hermitage, they were scared and soaked. Anne was sober. Bradley, the doorman, ran up to them holding a large umbrella. He escorted them up the marble stairs to the art deco lobby. They were both shaking.

"Ladies, are you all right?"

"No, no, we're not," said CC.

After the police left, Anne and CC sipped their tea in the lobby. When they had finished their tea, Bradley escorted them up to their suite. The hotel had upgraded them to compensate for their ordeal. There were fresh cookies and chocolates from the turndown service. Bradley ran a bath for Anne. As she soaked in the tub with classical music wafting over her, she inhaled the scent of burning sandalwood candles. The spicy fragrance relaxed her. She slid down the edge of the tub until her nose was just above the lavender-scented water.

While Anne bathed, CC sat at the writing desk, opening her iPad mini to review her photo gallery, trying to find a good photo for her blog. She wanted to keep her mind off the attack. There were plenty of shots from the Tobacco Barn, the Smoky Mountains and the Cherokee village. When she reached the end of the gallery, she stared at photos from the Naperville Last Fling. It made her sad thinking of the young Dave Southwell on the album cover she'd just purchased and remembering seeing the dead Dave Southwell on the stage. The last photo in the Naperville file was Roger's arm knocking down her camera. She enlarged the photo and saw a tattoo peeking around his elbow. It was a quarter note. As she enlarged it further, she could see there was something in the center of the note but she couldn't make it out. She ran to her bag and pulled out the Dave Southwell EP. On the back cover, the engineer's arm in the photo bore the same tattoo.

CC tapped on the bathroom door. "Anne, come out; I have to show you something."

Anne ignored her as she hummed along with Schubert's *Fifth.* She was thinking about Nigel. His British accent gave way to the beat of war drums. She thought about John Blackbear and slid her face under the water. Finally, Anne pulled herself out of the tub and put on the soft fleece bathrobe. She thought she could get used to living here. She liked being pampered.

She opened the door, stepping back into the room. "CC, I was trying to relax."

"Anne, you didn't hear me. Look at this. Dave Southwell's roadie Roger has the same tattoo as the sound engineer in this photo on the album I bought." CC handed Anne the album and her iPhone.

"So?" Anne sat down on the couch. "This is Nashville. I'm sure lots of people have music tattoos."

"Look closer. You can see a face in the note," CC said, pointing at both pictures again.

"So what?" Anne said, picking at the bonbons on the bed. "They both worked with Dave Southwell."

"Yeah, and Dave Southwell's dead," CC said. It might not be Pulitzer-worthy but she had sunk her teeth into a story and couldn't let it go.

"If you want to find out more, we can check out the two tattoo parlors on Broadway. I saw them when I was shopping earlier," Anne said, reaching for the fresh chocolate cookies. She took a nibble.

CC stared at the picture of Dave Southwell, rising country star, lead guitarist, singer, Nashville hunk—and now ghost.

Chapter Fifteen

The next day, they walked the now familiar three blocks from the Hermitage Hotel to Broadway. It was still early in the morning, and the streets were deserted. A street sweeper cleaned the debris from the night before. The Open sign in the 24-hour tattoo parlor window was flickering. CC opened the door. Taking out her handkerchief, Anne held the doorknob and closed it behind her. A young girl in short Daisy Dukes and cowboy boots decorated with sequined, brown crosses, sat in the barber-like tattoo chair. The tattoo artist was finishing the pink hummingbird tattoo on her shoulder.

He looked up at them and said, "I'll be right with you."

CC sat down in one of the chairs and watched him work. While she did not have any tattoos, she admired the art form. She turned to Anne and said, "He's really good. That hummingbird appears to be flying off her shoulder. It's almost 3D." CC stood up and stared at the images on the walls. "I wonder what kind of tattoo I would get." Nothing struck her fancy.

When the artist finished the girl's shoulder, she admired it in the mirror before paying him.

"Where'd you get those boots?" Anne asked the girl as she reached for the door handle.

"Down at Boot Barn. They were on sale." The girl smiled at Anne, before walking out the door.

"What would you like?" The artist handed them a black binder, which held pictures of tattoos encased in plastic sleeves.

CC skimmed through the book. She didn't see anything similar to the quarter note tattoo. She opened the photo gallery on her iPhone and showed him Roger's arm with the tattoo.

"I can draw something up like that."

"I can't make out the image on the quarter note," CC said.

The tattoo artist peered at the photo again. "I recognize that sleeve. It was an artist at the Rising Phoenix. I trained under him. That image in the note is a face."

"Whose face?"

He handed her back her phone. "I don't know."

"Whose the artist?" CC stuck the phone back in her backpack. "I'd like to know who to ask for when I go to the Phoenix."

"You can't. The Phoenix closed years ago. I don't know what happened to the artist."

Anne sat down in the tattoo chair. "I think I'd like something like an antique silver spoon." Found at a sale last year, it was one of Anne's most prized possessions.

CC shot her a withering look. "Not now, Anne, not now." She turned back to the tattoo artist. "Thanks for your help."

She pulled Anne out the door. Anne followed CC on the trek back to the hotel, planning her visit to Boot Barn later.

At the hotel, they retrieved the VW. "Betsy texted me about a music studio that's closed. She wants us to check it out." CC put the address in the GPS. It guided them to an industrial area that was surrounded by abandoned warehouses and factories. They pulled in front of the studio; the sign was falling off the brick front. It read West End Studios.

"Hey, Anne, this is where Dave Southwell recorded the album we bought," CC said, growing excited. She could feel the Pulitzer growing closer.

Anne couldn't imagine anything worthwhile inside. The building was dilapidated. It had been hit hard by the 2010 Nashville flood. The wooden door was warped, and the blue paint was peeling off. CC knocked and the door swung open by itself. The smell of mildew assaulted their nostrils.

On the floor was a crumpled up bright yellow condemned notice. "CC, do you think it's safe to be in here?" Anne asked.

"It's fine. Betsy wouldn't send us here if it wasn't safe," CC said.

"I wouldn't be so sure of that," Anne said, thinking about the china. Then she shook it off.

"The building's empty. It's going to be demolished. Betsy said that if we find anything, we can take it. Steven's company owns the property." CC paused a minute. "It's another part of history being torn down. This studio was a legend back in the day. And now, they're making room for multi-million dollar studios. The past is being torn down to make room for the future."

Anne tentatively took a step as CC reached up and pulled the string on the hanging light bulb. It didn't turn on. She made her way to the boarded up window and pulled on one of the 2 x 4 planks. "Give me a hand," she said.

Anne looked around the room and picked up a microphone stand. They pried off the window planks, releasing light into the room. Dust and mice scattered everywhere.

The front office of the studio held a reception desk, stacked high with papers and albums. The small 10 by 10 foot room was filled with microphone stands and old broken amplifiers.

"Anne, I think some of these old guitar amplifiers could be restored. That's a 1965 Fender blackface twin. It looks like it might have had some water damage but it's salvageable. Look at these mic stands. These are original, probably dating back to the 30s and 40s. They're rusty but we can clean them up."

Anne walked over to the corner. There was a mahogany sheet music cabinet. It had its original hardware but the Bakelite handle had been replaced with a mother of pearl knob shaped like a guitar. "I think this would be perfect for Steven's music room," Anne said. She'd even like it for herself.

She moved the cabinet back from the wall to check for the manufacturer's label. Behind it, leaning up against the wall was an old, tattered guitar case. The brass buckles were tarnished and worn away; the black covering was frayed. There were stickers from local bars—past and present. She unbuckled the case. The smell of moldy velvet hit her. She backed up for a second before gathering it up and bringing it outside to the fresh air. Its orange velvet lining showed marks from where the guitar had once been. *Darn, I was hoping the guitar would still be here*, Anne said to herself. She opened up the storage compartment. There was a blue leather guitar strap, some crumpled up paper and a cassette tape. "This is interesting," she said out loud. She left the guitar case outside and went back into the studio.

Hmm, I wonder where CC is, Anne thought, tiptoeing around the debris scattered across the floor. She felt something under her foot. Looking down, she saw an orange prescription bottle. She picked it up.

CC opened the glass door into the control room. She was disappointed to see that the mixing board was already gone. The reel to reels and tapes were missing as well. The recording room was emptied out except for the egg crate Styrofoam stapled to the walls. A moldy Persian rug was on the floor. Sound cables, guitar cords and beer cans were piled up on top of it. The ceiling was rotted through, and rain, which had started again, was pouring through. That's when she saw the cowboy boots sticking out from under the desk like the wicked witch except there were no munchkins around.

"Anne!" CC yelled.

Shoving the prescription bottle into her pocket, Anne ran into the room. She saw the man lying face down in a puddle. He had been dead for a while.

Anne ran out into the rain. Nashville wasn't working for her. She was ready to head home. CC followed her out. "CC, I'm done. I'm out of here. Last night and now this. Someone doesn't want us here," Anne said, stumbling over the guitar case.

"Anne, we're not going to be safe anywhere until we find out who that someone is." CC put her arm around her friend to comfort her.

Anne called Nigel. He arrived before the police and took Anne in his arms. He rocked her. *He was a very good Woody,* she thought, a hero, a real cowboy. She was tired of playing cowboys and Indians. She kissed him. "Anne, I'm taking you and CC back home. I'll handle the Nashville police," Nigel said. "It's not safe for you to be here anymore."

Nigel said everything Anne wanted to hear. All she wanted was to be home with her fat, white Persian, checking out estate sales online, watching eBay, listening to *Meet the Press* and making tea in Aunt Sybil's copper kettle. "Aunt Sybil?" she said out loud to Nigel's surprise. "I came here on a mission, a mission to rescue orphaned artifacts. To find homes for needful things. Aunt Sybil taught me to appreciate antiques for their beauty and for their history. I came here to do a job, and I'm going to finish it."

Nigel escorted them to the VW.

"Wait!" Anne said, pulling away. She grabbed the soaked guitar case, drained it and threw it in the back of the bus.

A short drive later, the cowboy, the chemist and the journalist sat together in the Nashville police station. "Trouble seems to follow you two around," Detective Clark said as he took their statements. He had been on duty the night before and had had the pleasure of interviewing the Spoon Sisters after the attack in the alley. "What were you doing at West End Studios today?"

"We were there to see if there was anything left to salvage for our client," CC said.

"We're antique hunters,' Anne interjected.

The police officer was not impressed. "That building is condemned. Everything of value has been removed. It's being torn down next week. Why would you go there?"

"Our client, Betsy Buttersworth, hired us to decorate her fiancée's house, and she overheard him talking about the studio and how items might still be left there. It's supposed to be a surprise."

"Who's her fiancé?"

"Steven Kendall."

Detective Clark appeared surprised. "You mean of Kendall Enterprises?"

Anne chirped up. "Yes, that's him."

Nigel put a hand on Anne's shoulder, interrupting her, "I'm Nigel Towers with the Chicago Police Department. These ladies are friends of mine. They helped me solve a very important case. I can vouch for them. You can contact my captain who can vouch for them also. Everything they are saying is true."

"I'll make some calls, and we'll verify. In the meantime, don't leave town. I may have additional questions," Detective Clark said, handing them a card with his phone number on it.

Nigel left the police station with Anne and CC. It was pouring rain again. They walked over to CC's VW. "You two head back to the hotel. I'm going to stay here and make sure everything is cleared up," he said, opening the door for Anne.

"Thanks, Nigel," Anne said.

CC started the VW.

"What do we do now? What's our next step?" Anne said.

"I think we need to talk to Steven Kendall."

They headed to the downtown office of Kendall Enterprises, located in a large steel building on Music Row. They walked through the revolving door and up to the receptionist. "We'd like to see Steven Kendall," CC said.

"Is he expecting you?"

"No, but he'll see us," Anne said. "We're friends of his fiancée, Betsy Buttersworth."

They sat down on the white leather couch, watching the beehive of activity. On the wall were pictures of country stars, authors, shopping malls, office buildings and hotels—a conglomerate of Kendall Enterprises' vast holdings. A short while later, Steven Kendall's assistant, a beautiful young brunette in a pencil skirt and silk blouse, walked over to Anne and CC.

"Steve said I should bring you up to his office. Follow me, please," she said.

Steven's office encompassed the entire twenty-second floor. The perky assistant opened the large double oak doors and ushered them into his office. "Mr. Kendall, they're here."

Anne wondered if she could ask the assistant where she got her blouse.

"Anne, CC, come in. What brings you to Nashville?" Steven Kendall put down the files in his hand, walking over to them. In his early fifties, he was distinguished with silver hair, a wide face and a chiseled jaw. He reminded CC of Betsy's second, no third, husband, old enough to keep her in comfort but young enough to keep her happy.

"We're doing some antique hunting for a client."

Steven smiled. "I know Betsy is planning to surprise me by decorating the coach house. We can keep that between us for now." His warm smile put both women at ease. He motioned for them to sit on one of the couches as he sat on the opposite one. His office had a southeastern motif with Native American artifacts. The dream catcher that hung next to the stainless fireplace was adorned with eagle feathers. Anne thought of John Blackbear and smiled.

"Can I offer you something to drink?" Steven asked.

Anne was about to open her mouth, but CC spoke first. "I'm sure you heard about West End Studios."

Steven's smile turned sour. "Yes, the police contacted me. My attorney had told Mr. Walters that he had to leave the premises after it was condemned. I had no idea he was still living there." Steven paused, and then said, "It must have been terrifying for you to find him like that."

"Yes, it was." Anne said with a little shiver.

"Walters? L. Walters?" CC asked.

"Yes, he owned West End Studios." Steven crossed his legs, one over another. "The flood bankrupted him. I bought the building, hoping that the money would help him get a new start. Walters was a respected engineer at one time. He will be missed by many." Steven sipped his coffee. "Are you going back to Chicago now?"

"We have more antique hunting to do," Anne said.

"Let me make it easy for you. I've got a lot of connections and I can give you an idea of what I like." He went to his desk and scribbled down some addresses and names. "You don't have to let Betsy know how you found these. Let her have her surprise."

Anne and CC thanked him and left. They sat in the VW bus, staring out the window. "Does it ever not rain in Nashville?" Anne asked.

She reached into her large orange Prada bag and pulled out some of the pages from the journal. "CC, I was reading this last night when I was in the tub." She read from Private Bement's journal, "As a private in the army, I was called upon in the relocation efforts to move the Cherokee from their home. Some attorneys argued to allow the Cherokee to remain in North Carolina. The friends I have made in the Oconfultee tribe of the Cherokee have been allowed to settle on a small reservation. There are many North Carolinians who are angered by this decision. I fear for my Cherokee friends. I fear what retribution may befall them." Anne paused as she reached into her large orange Prada bag to retrieve the rest of the journal. "I can't find where the next page of the story is. I'm going to have to sit down and put all the pages in order."

Anne put her bag behind her in the passenger seat and stared at the guitar case. She climbed over the seat and headed to the back.

"What are you doing?" CC asked.

"I want to show you something." Anne opened the case and took out the crumpled sheet music.

CC took the sheets of music from Anne and looked it over. "Most of these are ruined from the flood."

"This one is in very good condition. It was protected inside the compartment in the guitar case." Anne pulled out a piece of paper scribbled with musical notes. "There's a signature on the bottom."

CC took the pages from her. "This is all handwritten. I can't make out the name at the bottom. It's pretty badly smeared." CC thought for a moment. "I wonder what song this is," she said. "Brent's at the Bluebird tomorrow. Maybe he can play it for us."

Chapter Sixteen

CC pulled the bus into the small parking lot in front of the Bluebird Café. The small storefront music venue was known worldwide for launching the careers of some of country music's biggest stars. There was already a line out the door waiting to get in. CC maneuvered the VW into a tight parking space. Holding the door so it wouldn't hit the car next to her, Anne slid out onto the pavement. They walked up to the door. The bouncer stopped them and said, "Sorry, we're full. You can stand outside and listen."

"We're on the guest list," Anne said as she poked her head inside the door.

After searching the guest list and finding CC's name, he led them into the crowded space. It was small, and the chairs had been arranged in a circle around the little stage for Songwriter's Night. Waitresses weaved through the crowd.

Brent was standing by the bar. He recognized them and walked over. "Hi, I'm glad you came. Can I buy you a drink?"

"Sure. I'll have whatever you're having," CC said.

Anne hesitated and thought. *What sounded good? A margarita, a daiquiri?* Then she said, "I'll have a sea breeze."

"I'll be right back," Brent said. He walked over to the small bar in the corner and then returned to them balancing two drinks. "I'm going on next," he said.

CC smiled and watched Brent walk away. His jeans were tighter than what she'd remembered. She thought of a country song she'd heard some years ago. The line went something like, "I hate to see you leave but I love to watch you walk away." They sat at the tiny table. CC was not a fan of the new country music. She preferred classic country like Hank Williams, Patsy Cline and Loretta Lynn. She appreciated the simple structure of their songs and the storytelling.

Brent sat down on the stool on the small stage. He picked up his Gibson Hummingbird Acoustic and adjusted the mic. "How are ya'll today? I'm Brent Wilkins. I'd like to play a song that was my dad's favorite." He played the old George Jones' classic, "He Stopped Loving Her Today." CC got chills. His beautiful baritone voice filled the crowded room. Brent finished his three songs and walked back over to their table.

"You were great," CC said.

"Thank you. I'm playing at the Opry on Thursday night. I'd love to have you as my guest." Brent sat down at the table with them.

Anne wondered if the invitation included her. It would give her a chance to wear her new red cowboy boots that she'd found at Boot Barn after they'd left the tattoo parlor. "Excuse me," Anne said before walking away.

CC and Brent didn't notice her leave. "That's great, Brent. I'd love to hear more of your originals." CC leaned on her elbows and stared at him. "We've got a favor to ask you. Is there a quiet place we can talk?"

"My house is ten minutes from here. It's quiet."

Anne returned from the washroom and sat back down. "What's going on? What are you doing?" she asked when she saw CC standing up.

"We're going back to Brent's house."

Anne looked around the room, scanning the standing-room only crowd. "We've got a table." She checked her phone. “Plus, Nigel just texted me. I told him to come by.”

“Excuse me,” CC said to Brent. She grabbed Anne by the hand, pulling her into the corner. “Remember the whole point of coming tonight is to have Brent play the song for us.”

“Why don’t you go with Brent and have him play the song? I’ll wait here for Nigel. We’ll meet up later.”

CC agreed and left with Brent. Anne ordered another seabreeze and pulled out the journal pages. She was intrigued by the continuing saga of Private Bement. She began reading, “While the Cherokee have been granted permission to stay in North Carolina, the chief is still concerned for his people. I’ve grown very close to his daughter. I must confess my love to her, but I must keep it secret. I will meet her tonight during the ceremony of the new moon. I will tell her of my love and ask the chief for his permission for us to be wed. I fear that the townspeople will object—whites and Indians are not allowed to marry. I will take her across the Smoky Mountains into Tennessee to keep her safe.” Anne paused and said out loud to herself, “Ohmigod, it’s a love story.”

Chapter Seventeen

CC followed Brent to his little single-story house. He waited for her at the top of the steps on the porch. When she pulled up, he ran down the stairs and opened the car door. "Welcome." He took her hand as she got out of the VW. She was enjoying his attention.

The inside of the house looked like Brent—simple, efficient. She liked it. The couch was old but in good condition. The guitars were on stands throughout the living room. The house smelled like guitar polish and coffee. *Not unpleasant*, CC thought.

She sat down on the couch and crossed her legs. Brent plopped down next to her. He grabbed the guitar leaning up against the couch, a well-worn 1962 Martin tobacco sunburst. "This was my father's guitar. He toured with members of the Grand Ole Opry."

"Anne and I have tickets to see Thompson Square tomorrow. Holly Williams is opening for them. I loved her grandfather Hank. She's amazing too. She tours with John Hiatt. I love John Hiatt."

"My grandfather played with Hank Williams, Jr. He played backup to a lot of country legends. He played on the Opry stage, the original stage before the fire."

As Brent spoke, CC realized for the first time in a long time that she had feelings for another man besides Tony. Maybe it was more lust than love but either way she was attracted to him. Maybe it was his tight jeans. Maybe it was his music. CC broke her trance. "Oh, Brent." She reached into her purse, pulling out the crumpled papers. "We found this sheet music in a guitar case at West End Studios."

Brent took a look and recognized the scrawled signature. "I haven't seen that name in years."

"You can read it? Is he famous?"

"To Nashville people he is. He was a songwriter in the early days of the Opry. He was a street musician. I guess you'd call him homeless. I used to hear my grandfather talk about him; he was really talented. His name was Clarence Riddle." He put the sheet music onto the coffee table and picked up his guitar. Brent started playing a beautiful tapestry of sound. It was a haunting melody that felt familiar to CC.

"It's beautiful," CC said.

"It's a simple chord progression but it's really well written," he said. "Where'd you say you found this?"

"At the West End Studios." CC paused. "How come I've never heard of Clarence Riddle?"

"He disappeared back in the 1960s."

Chapter Eighteen

Anne dug deep into her large orange Prada bag. A lot of the journal pages were missing. She skimmed through the uneven handwriting, searching for anything about the officer and his Cherokee bride. "I arrived at the ceremony of the new year too late. My Cherokee friends had been killed by masked cowards. My love was dead." Anne stopped reading. *Oh, no, this is so sad*, she thought. Her eyes watered. She sipped her third sea breeze and then continued reading, "With her, dies my heart. The chief is mortally wounded. Right then, I swore my oath to avenge him and his daughter and his people. I will track these cowards down and justice will be delivered! The chief has entrusted me with his people's greatest treasure—the seven-pointed crystal of the morning star that is used for the holiest of ceremonies."

Anne stopped. She had to catch her breath. "He's talking about the original crystal that John Blackbear said was lost," she said out loud. Several people at the table next to her looked at Anne, sitting alone talking to herself. They inched their chairs slightly away from her. Anne downed her seabreeze and continued reading. All she could find in the remaining pages were more details of the killings.

The end of the journal—the last page—dated 1890, was hard to read. It was written in the shaky hand of an elderly man. "I lie on my deathbed with not many regrets. I've lived a good full life with a wife who was true. My son has grown to be a good Christian and has started his own family. I've watched Nashville grow from the small town I helped start into a thriving metropolis. My last words are 'I've kept my promise to my Cherokee brothers. I killed the man who killed my true love.'"

Anne looked up. "He lived in Nashville. I wonder if there is any record of him or his family." She walked out into the early evening air. The sun was setting. She dialed John Blackbear. "John, it's Anne. I've got information about the morning star crystal." As she spoke, the very tall and very British cowboy, Nigel Towers, appeared. Anne hung up the phone. "Nigel, it's so exciting! This journal is really a love story and—guess what?—I've got a clue on where to find the crystal."

Nigel listened politely not having a clue what she was talking about.

"I just told John Blackbear," Anne said with a giddy smile.

"Who?"

Anne realized that she couldn't put off this talk any longer. "You see, Nigel, I think you're great. Sweet. Funny."

"But . . ." Nigel interrupted.

"But I want us to be friends." She put her hand on his arm. "We are friends." Anne paused. "Just friends. I don't want anything to change our friendship. You're very dear to me. I don't want to lose you as a friend, but I don't have romantic feelings for you. I thought I did. You are so kind and funny and I love being with you. Maybe it's me, maybe it's us. I don't know but I can't make you wait around while I figure it out."

Nigel's face turned crestfallen. His question mark stature as he had bent down to be close to Anne became an exclamation point to accent the crushing news. He took his cowboy hat off suddenly feeling silly. "Anne, can I drive you home?"

"Don't you want to stay and hear the music? I have a table."

"I don't feel much like listening to music anymore."

Chapter Nineteen

The next morning, Anne awoke on her down-feathered custom-built five-diamond Hermitage luxury bed. At the sound of the room door opening, she looked over to the undisturbed queen bed next to hers. CC tip-toed into the room, closing the door quietly. Her walk of shame became a shuffle so as not to awake her friend. She took off the cowboy hat, revealing her disheveled soft brown hair. She was humming softly to herself.

Anne sat up in her bed, not wanting to ruin the show. She had never seen CC wear a cowboy hat.

CC's sundress was half unzipped in the back and she was carrying her high heels. Anne pulled the blanket up over her head not wanting to see the rest. She giggled under the sheets and pretended she was sleeping.

It was late afternoon when CC finally woke up. Anne was sitting in a lounge chair reading through the journal papers trying to find more information on the lost crystal. Bradley, the wonderful concierge, was standing next to her, pressing the French press coffee pot and pouring her a fresh cup. Anne had decided the day after they had arrived at the Hermitage that this was the lifestyle to which she was entitled. Unfortunately, she'd been born a hundred years too late. She was now living her gilded age; the Hermitage was frozen in 1910s opulence and gentility. Anne craved both. She also craved breakfast. She had grown hungry waiting for CC to wake up.

CC rubbed her eyes. "Oh, hi, Bradley."

"Ms. Muller, would you like some coffee?"

"Yes, that would be divine."

Bradley poured a cup into the Royal Doulton china and served CC in bed. "Ladies, will there be anything else? Late breakfast, early lunch?" he asked.

Before Anne could answer, CC said, "This will be just fine, Bradley. Thank you."

He exited through the door, carrying the silver coffee service.

After Bradley left, Anne said, "How'd things go at Brent's last night?" She held back her grin.

"Brent played the song on the sheet music. He recognized the signature of the songwriter too—Clarence Riddle. He was a street musician in Nashville in the 1960s. Brent's grandfather played with him when he was a budding songwriter."

"Oh, yeah, the song. How was the song?" Anne asked, sipping her coffee that she'd filled with fresh cream and four sugar cubes.

"It's a beautiful song. I can't help but feel I've heard it somewhere before," CC mused, sipping her coffee.

"Don't all country songs kind of sound the same?" Anne posed the rhetorical question. "Oh, CC, I forgot to tell you. Exciting news! I finished reading the journal. It's a love story. Well, a sad love story. Private Bement fell in love with the chief's daughter. She was murdered during the new moon ceremony. Remember? John Blackbear was telling us about the ceremony. It seems the chief gave Private Bement the crystal for safekeeping. After his the princess was murdered, he tracked down and killed her killer. He wound up moving to Nashville and dying here in 1890. We have to track down what happened to the crystal."

‘Let’s start with the archives at the *Nashville Tennessean*,” CC said. “We can look up information about Clarence Riddle and Private Bement.”

Chapter Twenty

The girls quickly dressed. The newspaper office was a few blocks away from the Hermitage. Bradley offered to walk with them and bring an umbrella in case it rained. "No, thank you," CC said before Anne could accept his help. CC was starting to worry about the bill and how much Bradley would cost by the time Anne was done. Then she wondered if Anne would ever be done with him.

Arriving at the newspaper office, CC explained their mission to the receptionist who led them to a small conference room, which contained microfilm of the newspaper's archives. CC scrolled through them until she came upon the papers from 1890. She scanned through, stopping when she found a brief obituary dated June 16, 1890. The obituary read, "Local business owner Randall Bement died of natural causes. He is survived by wife, Ada, and one son, Randall, Jr." There was no mention of his estate.

"When did his wife die?" Anne asked.

CC scrolled through the film looking for mention of Ada Bement. She found it in a later paper from 1901. "Look, Anne. Ada's obituary said she was survived by her son, Randall, Jr., who lives in North Carolina. It says here her estate will be handled by the firm of Goodlet and Sons."

"CC, keep looking; there has to be an advertisement for the estate sale."

Searching through the microfilm, CC found the advertisement in a paper from a few days later. In the ad, Goodlet and Sons announced the auction of the estate of Mrs. Randall Bement. Items highlighted included silver-plate, bone china and Indian artifacts.

"Indian artifacts? That's it!" Anne exclaimed. "That's it. It's got to include the crystal."

"We should look up Goodlet and Sons," CC said, making a note. She Googled their name. The company was still in business, advertising that they were a fourth-generation antiques and collectibles dealer with a booth at the Gaslight Antiques Mall near Vanderbilt University.

"We have to go," Anne insisted. "We can find antiques for Betsy. We can track down the crystal for John Blackbear."

"Hang on, Anne. Let me look up Clarence Riddle." CC returned the microfilm from the nineteenth century and pulled up the ones from the 1960s. She searched for anything related to the Opry. There were hundreds of photos and articles but no mention of Clarence Riddle. "Let me try Brent's grandfather, Wilkins."

"This is taking so long. Isn't this all computerized?" Anne asked, thinking about getting to the Gaslight.

"I like looking this way. It's original. Something could have been lost when they scanned it. Plus, I like the feel of the machine." CC spun the dial of the microfilm like a seasoned slot machine player.

She finally came to a series of black and white photographs from 1968. There were several musicians standing outside the Ryman Auditorium. The caption read, "Hank Williams, Jr., Johnny Cash, Dickel Wilkins." "Hey, that's Brent's grandfather!" CC could see the family resemblance. The fourth person was named Clarence Riddle. "That's him!" The picture was grainy but she now knew what Riddle looked like. He looked familiar but she couldn't place the face.

Anne peered over CC's shoulder. "Hey, that looks like my guitar case. Does it say anything more about him?"

"No, just his name. That's it. There's no other information."

"Can we go now? Can we go to the Gaslight?" Anne had already looked at the antique store's website for its hours. She had put the address into her Google maps. She was primed and ready for the hunt. She had the scent.

"Let's get something to eat before we head there. I'm starving," CC said as she returned the microfilm to the receptionist.

"Bradley packed us a lunch," Anne said as they left the newspaper office. They sat on a wooden bench outside. Anne pulled two elegantly wrapped paper bags out of her Prada bag. Bradley had taken fresh-baked bread and precisely cut the crusts. Inside the bread was honey-cured ham with Gouda and an herb-infused mayonnaise. There were also linen napkins encased in bone china napkin rings and a small bottle of sparkling water. CC just stared. "I love Bradley," Anne said. CC thought about the bill once again.

After lunch, they walked back to the Hermitage and retrieved the VW from the parking garage. Bradley had the valet wash it and placed two bottled waters in the cup holders. Anne fought the urge to hug and kiss him. CC worried her friend was getting spoiled. She would be even harder to live with after this Bradley treatment.

They followed the GPS, which led them to a Staples parking lot. "This is strange," Anne said. "I think the address must be wrong." She looked around and around, craning her head this way and that until she caught a glimpse of an old fashioned gaslight and a sign with an arrow pointing around the corner. "There it is!" she proclaimed with a sigh of relief.

CC parked the bus and Anne jumped out of it. They entered the building. Anne immediately felt at home. She thought to herself, *Nashville isn't that bad.* The antique store was on the second level. Portraits were displayed on the wall of the staircase. She could feel the eyes follow her as she made her ascent. Anne stopped to admire them. Then she continued her climb up the stairway to heaven. She stopped at the top to catch her breath. In a raspy voice, she said, "Treadmill."

"What? What did you say?" CC asked.

Anne waved her off. "Nothing." She scanned the row after row of cluttered antiques. This was definitely familiar territory. The first booths held enormous collections of jewelry, silver-plate and rare Rookwood pottery.

As she moved farther into the mall, she found themed booths. One booth held all music antiques. Her eyes were immediately drawn to a turn of the century music stand that had a twisted wrought iron base and a solid oak top. A brass bar used to hold the sheet music in place was absolutely gorgeous. "CC, come here. This would be great for Betsy," Anne said, looking at the price tag.

In the same booth, there was a 1920s Zenith tabletop radio. There was a Gibson resonator guitar in excellent condition with mother of pearl fret inlays. "Look at this, CC." Anne pointed out all the items, including an oil painting of some of the Grand Ole Opry stars. In a glass case, there was a signed letter from Johnny Cash to an old friend. The first paragraph was the actual lyrics to "I've been Everywhere." "We have to buy this booth, CC," Anne enthused.

"Anne, calm down; we don't want them to know that we're excited," CC said.

"Oh, look! There's an old cassette player. Let's get that, too, so we can listen to the tape." Anne pointed to a corner where the small cassette deck sat.

"What cassette tape?" CC asked.

"The one that was in the guitar case."

The girls negotiated with the store manager to purchase the whole booth. They then continued browsing up and down the aisles. Anne wandered to whatever caught her fancy but was still careful not to miss anything. CC went in a more precise line. She found the Goodlet and Sons booth. It filled a whole corner of the room with a large black and white sign that read, "Goodlet and Sons, Fine Antiquities." She called Anne over.

The booth contained all of Anne's favorite things—fine china, silver and beautiful crystal. Anne's eyes were drawn to a low art deco brass planter still with its original insert that matched the one that she carried in her purse, now for protection. It had served her well. She admired the gilded lady who adorned both sides and felt its heavy weight under her hand. This would have to be added to her personal collection.

Next she found a matching set of 1920 brass Viking book ends depicting ships at sea. She had been watching a similar set on eBay but these were in great condition and better priced. She picked those up, too. Her arm was starting to get heavy from the weight of her large bag. She looked around for help but couldn't find any. She thought about calling Bradley, but CC would probably yell at her.

Just when she thought she'd seen every item in every nook and cranny, she saw something sparkle in the corner cabinet where the sunlight burst through the tempered glass skylight. She moved three large rolled-up oriental rugs that were leaning against a small curio cabinet. And there it was—unassuming, underpriced, perfect. The tag read simply, “Crystal, $5.” Anne picked up the seven-pointed morning star crystal. She closed her eyes; she imagined Private Bement under a full moon, his saber drawn fighting off masked marauders, defending his Indian princess. She felt the power of the morning star crystal that she was holding––the most sacred artifact of the Cherokee people. She felt John Blackbear’s strong arms around her. The rapid beating of her heart sounded like the beating of war drums in her head.

Chapter Twenty-one

CC pulled the VW in front of Brent's house and parked on the street. He was sitting on the porch playing guitar. As they sauntered up the walkway, Anne whispered, "He is really cute."

"Sshh," CC said, balancing the cassette deck in her arms.

"Come on in." Brent stood up and took the deck out from CC. He opened the door with his foot. CC walked in followed by Anne.

Anne looked around the small house. It was serviceable.

Brent set the cassette deck on his dining room table and grabbed two bookshelf speakers and a small power amp. After he was done setting everything up, CC handed him the cassette tape. He held it for a moment. "I haven't seen one of these in a while. You found it in the guitar case with the sheet music?" He turned the cassette over in his hands; it said, "West End Studios" with the initials CR added. He took a pencil and unwound the tape, straightening out the tangles and then tightened it again. He put it in the tape deck, turned it on and sat down next to CC at the dining room table. They all stared at the tape deck as if they were watching a show on the television, waiting for something to happen.

The tape hissed and popped. After several seconds, they heard Clarence Riddle talking to Walter, the sound engineer.

"Walter, can you bring the guitar up a little louder in the headphones?" they heard.

"Will do, Clarence," was the reply.

Then Clarence played "Young Hearts." After three and a half minutes, the tape hissed and popped, then tangled and locked. Brent stopped the tape deck. Anne, CC and Brent stared at each other, not speaking. After what seemed like hours, Brent pulled the tape out and eyed it again. "This says 1968," he said. "That's almost 50 years *before* Dave Southwell wrote, recorded and performed his biggest hit song—that song."

"Are you saying that Dave Southwell stole this song?" Anne asked.

"Yeah, note for note," Brent said.

Chapter Twenty-two

Anne sat in the lobby of the Hermitage waiting for John Blackbear. Balancing a silver service, Bradley brought her tea and cookies. "It looks like another rainy day, Miss Hillstrom. Will you be leaving? Do you need an umbrella?"

"No, Bradley. I'm waiting for someone." Anne picked up one of the sugar cookies.

"Can I bring you anything else?"

"It's rather cold in here."

Bradley smiled. "Yes, the joke is that if you're in Nashville and you're going to the movies, don't forget your coat. We like to turn the air conditioning up to get rid of the humidity." He returned a short while later with a pashmina shawl that he wrapped around her shoulders.

"Bradley, this is lovely." Anne felt the soft wool and eyed the beautiful paisley pattern. She wondered how much it cost.

"It's available for sale in the gift shop, but you can use it for now."

"Thank you, Bradley. That lunch yesterday was delicious."

"Can I ask the chef to fix you something?"

Anne looked around to make sure CC wasn't within earshot. "I would love a plate of pecan pancakes with warm maple syrup. And some sugar cured ham if it's not too much trouble."

Bradley smiled. "I'll bring it over shortly."

Anne sat back in the oversized chair and stared up at the stained glass mosaic ceiling. It had been restored to its original 1910 beauty. The crystal chandeliers gleamed in the morning light. There was more marble in this gorgeous lobby than in an Italian quarry. *Yes, this is I where I am meant to be, she thought. A hundred years later or now, I can live this lifestyle. Just me and Bradley and the occasional visit from John Blackbear.*

As she finished her last piece of sugar cured ham and sipped her fresh-squeezed orange juice, she heard footsteps coming up the stairs that split the main floor from the lobby. All she could see was the top of the pointy head that she recognized to be the very tall and no longer cowboy, Nigel Towers. He walked up to Anne and pointed to the chair across from her, motioning for approval to sit down. She nodded.

He sat down, bumping his knee on the edge of the Chippendale table. "Anne, I wanted to say goodbye before I head back to Chicago. I thought about what you said. I'm sorry things couldn't work out between us. But I want you to know that your friendship is important to me. If all we can be is friends, then that's all there is to say about that." He managed a slight half smile, touched her hand and walked off.

As he walked down the stairs, John Blackbear was walking up. The two glanced at each other sideways, without recognition. Nigel gave the chief a polite nod and left the Hermitage.

When he reached Anne, John Blackbear knelt down and kissed her on the cheek, and then sat down across from her in the chair Nigel had just vacated. "Anne, it was so good to hear from you. It's good to see you again."

Anne smiled and nodded.

"On the phone, you said you had a lead on the morning star crystal. . ."

Anne stopped him. She couldn't contain herself any longer. She reached into her large orange Prada bag and retrieved the morning star crystal that was wrapped in tissue paper. She placed it in the middle of the table and unwrapped it with a flourish as though it was the Holy Grail.

John Blackbear stared, not believing his eyes. "Anne, is this truly the morning star crystal?" He picked it up and held it up to the morning light. The seven points glistened and glowed. John Blackbear retrieved his iPhone and brought up the picture of the drawing from 1830. It appeared to be the exact piece, even down to the impurities in the crystals that lined up with the one in the photo like a road map. "Anne this is remarkable. This is our morning star crystal! How did you find it?"

"I'm an antique hunter. That's what I do." Anne sat back and sipped her Irish coffee.

Chapter Twenty-three

The black Lincoln town car pulled up in front of the Ryman Auditorium. Bradley jumped out of the driver's seat and opened the rear door. Anne stepped out, handing him her empty water bottle. "Thank you, Bradley. We will call you when we're done."

Bradley nodded and smiled.

CC and Anne walked into the original home of the Grand Ole Opry. They paid their admission fee and entered the exhibit area. They paused to look at the display of Minnie Pearl's shoes and her straw hat with the price tag still attached. Hank Williams' sequined white jacket hung in a sealed case. When they came to the early photos, they found what they were looking for—the 1960s exhibit area.

A photograph showed Jimmy Dickens and Merle Haggard on stage. Beyond them, in the wings was a well-dressed man holding a cigar. His arm was around Clarence Riddle's shoulder. Another man stood next to them, smiling. Riddle was wearing tattered overalls and holding a Martin guitar. Neither were identified in the caption but Anne and CC recognized Riddle from the photo they'd seen before.

"This photo is much clearer than the microfiche photo. Maybe we can speak to the curator and find out who Clarence is speaking to," CC said.

CC showed her press pass to one of the tour guides and asked to speak to the curator. They waited for an hour. While they waited, Anne viewed the history of women's costumes from the Opry and was drawn to a yellow sequined dress once worn by Loretta Lynn. Finally, a little white-haired lady came up to them. "I'm Sarah Cummings, curator. I heard you were writing an article and wanted some information. What newspaper are you with?"

CC coughed and hesitated. "Actually, I'm a freelancer. I'm researching a story about the early days of the Ryman. I saw an interesting photograph of Merle Haggard on stage. I wanted to find out who the three men watching in the wings are."

Sarah took the glasses that were hanging from a chain around her neck and put them on her nose. She examined the photo closely. "I don't know who the little guy in the overalls is. The well-dressed man is Colonel Anderson. He was a record producer. The other man is Sam Hopkins who was a staff songwriter for the Colonel's record company. He wrote many hits for some of the biggest artists that got their start at the Ryman including," Sarah took another look at the photo. "Merle Haggard."

"That's really interesting. Are they still around?" CC asked.

"Colonel Anderson retired years ago. Hopkins still has an office on Music Row." Sarah pointedly looked at her watch. "What else can I tell you about the Opry?"

"Nothing really. I think that's all we needed," CC said.

Anne turned to Sarah and asked. "Are any of these dresses for sale?" She pointed at the Loretta Lynn collection.

Sarah frowned. "Absolutely not."

Chapter Twenty-four

They drove along Music Row, a side street of assorted residential houses that had been renovated into music production companies and recording studios. Many had signs out front with names like Frog Recording, Late in the Game Records and Blue Bayou Productions. They stopped when they reached Hopkins' Publishing, one of the smaller houses on the Row. Even before they got out of the car, they could hear the guitar through the open screen door. Anne and CC walked up the steps. They knocked until the guitar finally stopped. Sam Hopkins limped to the door, using a cane. "Can I help you?" he asked.

"Mr. Hopkins, I'm CC Muller, a journalist."

"Journalist? What do you want with me?" Hopkins leaned against the doorjamb.

"I'm writing an article about Clarence Riddle. Sarah, the curator at the Opry, gave me your name. I wondered if we could talk to you," CC said, pulling out her press pass.

"Sure. Come on in." He held open the screen door, leading them into a living room that he had converted into a recording studio.

"Did you work with Clarence?" CC asked, sitting down and pulling out her reporter's notebook. "I understand you were a staff songwriter for Anderson Records."

Mr. Hopkins rubbed his stubby beard and gave a husky laugh. "Anderson, that son of a bitch! I haven't thought about him in years."

Anne looked around at the pictures of all the artists on the wall. She recognized many of them. Scattered around the room was Hopkins' collection of musical instruments including a fiddle on an end table. She went up to it to take a closer look. It was signed by the cast of *Hee Haw*. "This is very cool. You wouldn't consider selling this, would you?"

Mr. Hopkins didn't acknowledge her. "To be fair, Colonel Anderson gave me my start. I was hanging around the Opry like every other wanna be. I was mostly what you'd call nowadays a street musician, playing for pennies. I wasn't that good," Hopkins said. "Clarence was the real talent."

"Can you tell me more about Clarence?" CC asked.

"Clarence was a genius. Everything I learned about song structure and chord progression, I learned from him. He took me under his wing. Whenever he made enough money to get a room for the night, he'd let me crash."

"Did Clarence work for Anderson Records?"

"Oh no; he wanted nothing to do with Colonel Anderson. He was a loner. All he wanted to do was drink and write songs. That's probably what killed him—the alcohol. When he wasn't drunk, he was a hell of a songwriter."

CC pulled out the sheet music and showed it to Hopkins. He picked up his guitar and started playing. "I remember this song. That's my handwriting."

"Your handwriting?" CC asked.

"Clarence was illiterate, and he couldn't write a lick of music. He would play a song for me, and I would write the lyrics and music out for him."

"How could he sign his name?"

"I signed it for him. I wanted him to get credit. It was a good song." He looked at the sheet music and smiled. "That's his blue fingerprint on there."

CC hadn't noticed the blue smudge before. She peered closer.

"When he couldn't make enough money playing on the street, Clarence would pick blueberries as a day worker. His hands would be stained for days. It would get all over his guitar. That's how he got his nickname, *Blue Note*." Hopkins chuckled at the memory.

"What happened to Clarence?" CC asked.

"I don't know. Nobody knows. He just disappeared one day. He was always off on benders, missing for days," he said.

"Didn't anyone look for him? What about the police?"

"You have to understand that Clarence was homeless, drunk and a bit crazy. Not the type who people look for. I went to the police, filed a missing persons report. The last place I saw him was at West End Studios. He was recording with Walters."

"L. Walters, the sound engineer?"

"Yeah, Walters did all of the Colonel's recording in the early days. Clarence would hang around the studio and play backup for drinks or recording time." Hopkins paused. "Shame about Walters. I'd lost touch with him. I didn't even know he died until I read about it in the papers."

"Who else worked for the Colonel?" CC asked.

"A lot of staff writers. None of them any good. All the hits were Clarence's. We just wrote them down and the Colonel took credit for them. He paid Clarence in whiskey."

"I'd like to learn more about Clarence Riddle? Is there anyone else I could talk to?" CC asked.

"Clarence had an older brother, Jeremiah. I only saw him once. He was shipped out to Vietnam in '67. When he came back, he was pretty screwed up from the war. He tore up the town looking for Clarence."

"He never found him?"

Hopkins shook his head. "Clarence just disappeared. Rumor was he drank himself to death. If he did, they never found the body. Jeremiah moved to California, somewhere near L.A."

"Do you know how I could reach him?" CC asked.

Hopkins shook his head.

Thank you for your time." CC stood up, followed by Anne.

"Are you sure you won't consider selling the fiddle?" Anne asked one last time.

Hopkins shook his head and smiled.

Chapter Twenty-five

CC and Anne sat in the VW bus outside of Hopkins' house. CC made a phone call. "Hi, Ted, it's CC." She paused for a moment. "I'm good. I'm in Nashville, working on a story and I need your help. Can you track down a Jeremiah Riddle? He's in his 70s, Vietnam vet. Originally from Nashville. Anything you can find. I'm trying to get a phone number. I owe you dinner next time I'm out there." CC hung up the phone and started the VW.

"Aren't you going to tell me who that was?" Anne said.

"It was my friend, a former colleague, Ted Nobokiv. He's an investigative reporter for the *LA Times*. If Jeremiah Riddle lives in California and is still alive, Ted will track him down."

"Where to now?"

"Nashville coroner's office." CC put the address in the GPS and started driving.

Anne had no response for that. She sat back and sipped on her Diet Coke. She wished she'd asked Bradley to pack her a snack. She was getting hungry.

It was late afternoon, and there was no parking around city hall. CC was tired of paying for parking everywhere. It wasn't just the parking; it was the valet, and the tips for the valet. It went against her grain as a frugal German pragmatist. She circled the block for twenty minutes until she found some street metered parking. Anne took out her change bag and fed quarters to the hungry machine.

Entering the building, they paused to eye the office listing board; the coroner's office was located on the ninth floor. Both elevators had yellow "out of service" signs on them. Anne's heart stopped at the sight. "Come on; we have to take the stairs," CC said, opening the door to the stairwell.

"You're kidding. It's nine floors. You can do that. I'll wait here." Anne pointed to a bench along the wall.

"You're coming with me," CC said, pulling her into the stairwell.

By the time, they reached the third flight of stairs, Anne was mumbling, "treadmill." When they reached the seventh floor, she said something about Bradley under her breath. CC couldn't make it out. They finally reached the ninth floor in time to hear the ding of the elevator door opening. It had been fixed. Anne took a lace handkerchief out of her bag and wiped her dripping brow. She leaned against the door and panted.

The glass door was etched with the words *Nashville City Coroner*. They went inside and a young woman behind the counter, greeted them. "May I help you?"

CC showed her press pass. "I want some information on a Mr. Walters. He passed away two days ago."

The young woman clicked something on her computer. "This is a police investigation. We're not allowed to release any information."

By the stern look that the young woman gave CC, she knew not to ask any further. "I understand. I'll contact the police department. Thank you."

They walked back out into the hall. "Anne, you're going to have to call Nigel."

"CC, I can't," Anne protested.

"What do you mean you can't?"

"You're the one who urged me to have the talk with Nigel to tell him how I really felt, so I did. He left town. I haven't spoken with him since."

"Anne, this is business. It's important. It's the only way we're going to get information about Walters."

Reluctantly, Anne agreed. She took out her iPhone but there was no service in the building. She pressed the button for the elevator. It did not light up. She pressed it again with the same result. "Oh, great; you gotta be kidding me."

They took the stairs—CC two at a time; Anne holding the railing, huffing and puffing. They reached the lobby in time to hear the ding of the elevator doors open as people got on.

Anne tried the phone again as she walked outside the building. A gentle mist started. "Nigel, can you hear me? I'm sorry to bother you but I could use your help." She put her hand over the phone. "CC, what am I supposed to be asking him?"

"Tell him we want a copy of Walters' autopsy report," CC said.

Anne relayed the information to Nigel. She thanked him and hung up.

"Is he going to do it?"

"Yes," Anne replied. "Can we go eat now?"

They walked the five blocks back to the VW. Anne was sweating in the humid air. She wasn't used to this much humidity in the fall.

CC started the bus. "We're heading to see a man about Demonbreun."

Chapter Twenty-six

They arrived at the country home of one of Tennessee's largest collectors of Nashborough history, Pierre Robertson. The large country estate was located 20 minutes outside of Nashville, near the Cumberland River—the original site of the founding of Nashville by Timothy Demonbreun. "You know, Anne," CC said. "Timothy Demonbreun was French-Canadian and was the first white settler here in 1769. He established a fur trading post that he could use for his trapping expeditions."

Anne wasn't terribly excited. These weren't going to be pretty antiques. She liked shiny things. "How did you find out about this collector?"

"From Bradley."

Anne smiled and said, "Ahhh, Bradley." She wished she had that sandwich now.

They were greeted at the wrought-iron double doors by a butler. He led them into the two-story foyer, which was comprised of beautiful antiques dating back to the 1700s. Anne marveled at the exquisite décor. She couldn't have done better herself. She wondered if any of this collection was for sale.

The butler walked the ladies into the sitting room where Mr. Robertson was waiting. He was wearing a fringed, deerskin Daniel Boone jacket and matching boots. *Probably original*, Anne thought.

"Welcome to my home." He put down the instrument in his lap and stood up to greet them. "My friend, Bradley, contacted me and said you wanted to see my collection. Are you interested in Tennessee history?"

"In particular, Nashville," CC said.

Anne interrupted. "We're antique hunters." She handed him a card.

CC stopped her and said, "We have a client who is decorating her house for her fiancé. He's a very influential businessman in Nashville. We've been commissioned to find pieces for his collection. Bradley spoke highly of you and said you had an amazing collection. Specifically, we're looking for anything related to Timothy Demonbruen."

"You're familiar with our local history. He was a very interesting pioneer," Mr. Robertson said. "He lived in a cave just downstream from here for months while he was building his home."

"I heard that. Is his original homestead still around?" CC asked.

"Not much of it. I can show you the site," Robertson said.

"You know, Anne, Demonbreun served as lieutenant governor at Fort Kaskaskia in Illinois. He had a family there," CC said.

"And he had a second one here in Nashville. He had five children with his Illinois wife and four with his Nashville mistress," Mr. Robertson said. "He established a mercantile and fur trading business and had 17 employees." He led them into a back room. "Here is one of the early advertisements for his store."

The cluttered, framed newspaper ad announced a business location on *Public Square* and listed window glass, paper, cured deer hides and buffalo tongues. "Later on, he opened a tavern," Mr. Robertson said. "He loved music. This is his original hurdy gurdy." Robertson held up an instrument that was lying on a wood table. He demonstrated how to play it.

"You know, Anne, the crank on a hurdy gurdy makes a sound just like a bow on a violin," CC said. "Would you consider selling any of these items?"

"Oh, no, this collection is dear to me. I could never part with any of it."

"You know, the gentleman we're buying for works in the music industry. Not only has his family been in Nashville for generations, but he also works with famous musicians. I think he'd appreciate the history of the hurdy gurdy and perhaps use it on recordings that would be heard by millions of country fans."

Mr. Robertson thought. "I enjoy beautiful things. I cherish them. I want others to appreciate the history and the beauty also. If this hurdy gurdy can be shared with other enthusiasts, I would part with it."

While Mr. Robertson and CC were talking, Anne was mesmerized by an ormolu music box. She opened it and cranked it. Its tinkling tune filled the room. Both Mr. Robertson and CC turned to look at her. "That was a gift to my grandmother from my grandfather when he came back from France in 1922. It was her engagement present," Mr. Robertson said.

Anne set the music box back down carefully. Even she couldn't ask him to give up a family heirloom.

They paid for the hurdy gurdy and an early map of Nashville. "Thank you, Mr. Robertson."

"If you're interested in music antiques, you should come to the reception that I'm hosting tomorrow for the Nashville Historical Society at Andrew Jackson's Hermitage plantation," Mr. Robertson said, as he escorted them to the front door. "Colonel Anderson will be attending. He was very influential in the early days of Nashville music. I'm sure you would find him fascinating."

Anne and CC looked at each other.

“It’s a period ball celebrating Andrew Jackson’s legacy. I will let Bradley know to add you to the guest list.”

“Is Bradley part of the historical society?” Anne asked.

“Everyone in Nashville knows Bradley. When you need something, you ask Bradley.”

Anne nodded in agreement. “Thank you so much, Mr. Robertson,” Anne said. “We will definitely see you tomorrow evening.” Anne got in the car and pondered about her costume. Now she wished she’d borrowed Aunt Sybil’s brooch from her cousin, Susan. “This is great. I wanted to tour the estate anyway. Now we can do it for free. I’ll call Bradley.”

Chapter Twenty-seven

The black Lincoln town car pulled up in front of Monique's, a vintage clothier located off a side street, one block away from Broadway. Bradley jumped out of the driver's seat and opened the door for Anne and CC. "Ladies, do you want to me to come in with you? I know the owner."

"Of course, Bradley," Anne said. She definitely was getting used to this service. All CC saw was dollar signs.

Walking ahead of them, Bradley opened the door that led into the small storefront. The window display contained stage costumes from different decades. "Monique's is mostly known for its country stage costumes, but the owner also deals in high-end vintage clothing in her Charleston store. I contacted her yesterday. She had ball gowns overnighted that she thinks will work for you."

As they spoke, a beautiful woman floated into the room wearing a classic Diane von Furstenberg wrap dress and pearls. Her jewels were vintage Harry Winston. Anne could tell they were not imitation. She was pleased to be in such elegant company and wondered if she could try the necklace on. Anne thought Monique resembled Helen Mirren.

Bradley kissed Monique on both cheeks and spoke rapidly in French. Anne and CC watched in amazement at being exposed to another one of Bradley's talents. "This is Monique. Monique, may I introduce Ms. Hillstrom and Ms. Muller. They are antique hunters," Bradley explained with a flourish.

Anne curtseyed as if she were in the royal court. CC shook Monique's hand. With a lilting French accent, Monique spoke, "I understand you ladies have been invited to tomorrow's charity ball at the Hermitage plantation. You will need the right attire for the costume ball. I have the perfect gowns for you both. I believe Bradley was correct in estimating your measurements. For you, Miss Hillstrom." Monique held up a royal purple silk gown with a bustle and layers and layers of flounces.

Anne smiled approvingly and reached out a hand to touch the silk. Her fairy godmother had picked the perfect gown. She already felt like Cinderella.

"And, for you, Miss Muller, a more practical gown." Monique held up a severe high-necked teal satin ball gown.

Reaching for the hanger of the purple dress, Anne could feel the history emanating from it. "Are these authentic dresses from the era?"

"Of course. That dress you're holding was worn by General Nash's wife at a similar ball at Mr. Jackson's house. And, the one you hold, Ms. Muller, was worn by a French countess—Dubuque—who was a mistress of Mr. Jackson's, or so the story goes. Quite scandalous, wouldn't you agree?"

Before Monique could finish, Anne was in the dressing room changing. She was a bit worried since she had been off her South Beach, low carb, paleo, Weight Watchers diets. Oh, what the heck! She was off all her diets, but she wore her Fitbit faithfully everyday and tried to reach her 10,000—more like 2,000—step quota. *This vacation—no correction*, Anne thought, *antique hunting trip, had not been kind to any of her diets, and she could see a slight difference in her waistline.*

She slid the gown on and felt the smooth silk slide over her. It fit perfectly. Bradley was amazing. She twirled around and watched the silk float like an exuberant butterfly around her ankles. This was her destiny. She had found her time machine and this evening would be set for 1820.

CC stared at the full-length gold-gilded mirror. She wouldn't say it out loud and she was embarrassed to think it, but she looked beautiful. She had felt beautiful ever since the night at Brent's house. She no longer thought about Tony or Italy or her ex-husband. She felt like Mata Hari using her feminine wiles to spy on the enemy. But who was the enemy?

Bradley kissed both Monique's cheeks, spoke again for several minutes in French as the two laughed. Anne looked around the shop, admiring the sequined jackets, short leather skirts and bandana tie-dyed halter tops—all fitting for a stage performance. "Monique will have the gowns pressed and then delivered to the hotel," Bradley said.

As they left Monique's, Anne received a text message on her iPhone from Nigel. It read "glad to help." She opened the attachment. Anne downloaded the police report. She skimmed it, stopping at the sentence that read, "Victim had tattoo of blue quarter note on his arm." They looked at each other. The police report confirmed what they already knew. Walters had the same tattoo as Roger.

CC read over her shoulder. They both were silent.

Chapter Twenty-eight

Bradley pulled the 1940s maroon Duesenberg up the long driveway leading to Andrew Jackson's majestic Hermitage plantation. Its oil lanterns were aglow in the early evening. In the circular driveway, there were limousines, Rolls Royce's and exotic sports cars. For the occasion, Bradley had borrowed the car from a local collector and had donned full chauffeur attire. The front entrance was a cluster of activity, a rainbow of color from the array of period gowns. Almost everyone stopped to watch as the million-dollar car pulled up by the front steps. All the Nashville elite wanted to see who would step out. Bradley exited the driver's seat, placed his chauffeur's cap on his head, opened the back door, clicked his heels and bowed. He reached his hand down to first help Anne out and then CC. As he bowed his head, he gave them a wink.

Around her neck, Anne was wearing a gold and ivory cameo locket; Bradley had borrowed it from a turn-of-the-century jewelry display in the hotel's lobby. CC was wearing a pearl and emerald choker from the same collection. Apparently, there was no limit to Bradley's skills.

Anne and CC walked up the steps, nodding at the gawking Nashvillians. From the ballroom, they could hear the opening strains of a waltz. They crossed over the lobby and wandered through the crowd into the ballroom. Anne felt like she had stepped back in time to antebellum days. She imagined Andrew Jackson walking down the marble staircase. The beauty and elegance of the young country, this young city displaying its potential.

Anne strolled around, touching all the antiques. It was a rare opportunity to view history from the other end of the red velvet rope. From behind her, she heard a familiar voice. She turned to see Chief John Blackbear wearing full tribal chieftain dress. "John, what are you doing here?"

He smiled. "I am representing the seven clans of the Cherokee who were allowed to stay in North Carolina. President Jackson enforced the Indian Removal Act but was persuaded to allow our clans to stay in North Carolina."

Anne was so excited she forgot her decorum and kissed his cheek. John Blackbear's smile grew. "Anne, I must talk to you. Can we walk out to the veranda?"

The early evening fall air was cool and crisp, but not cold. The wind coming off the rolling hills blew through Anne's golden hair. Her bare shoulders glistened ivory in the waning moon. Her blue eyes sparkled. John Blackbear towered over her like the great mountain of a man he was. His eyes were soft and his voice gentle. "Anne, I met with the leaders of the seven clans. The morning star crystal as you know is invaluable to my people. They wish that I not only thank you for finding it, but that I give you this. I was going to bring it to your hotel, but now please take it." He handed her an envelope embossed with the casino logo.

"John, what is this? I didn't do this for any reward. I wanted to help you. I care about you. I understand the importance of preserving history." She tried to hand the envelope back to him.

"Anne, the casino has been very profitable. Money is not an issue for my people. This is merely our way of thanking you. I insist. Do with it what you wish, but to refuse it would be an insult to the clans." John's hand reached over hers, pushing the envelope back toward her.

"Thank you, John." She placed the envelope in her bag. Anne reached up and put her arms around John Blackbear's neck and pulled him down. She kissed him once as a thank you. The second kiss was all for her.

While Anne and Chief Blackbear lingered in the moonlight, CC was in a group of history professors from Vanderbilt who were discussing Andrew Jackson's policy on tobacco reform. "You know, Andrew Jackson was one of the first to introduce a natural tobacco pesticide to fight aphids," CC broke into their conversation. "He learned the recipe from the Cherokee Indians who used it for their corn crops. It transferred quite nicely to tobacco crops. The Cherokee called it kaola. It was a mixture of burnt chestnut tree bark, tickseed leaves, and sage. I forget the rest, but I can send you the recipe if you're interested. I've actually made it for my garden back home in Glen Ellyn, Illinois. I make a paste that I mix with three to one fertilizer. Then I bury it deep in the roots of my tomato plants and other herbs in early spring. It works quite well."

The professors silently stared at her, wondering who she was and why she was talking to them. The band stopped and the caller announced "Ladies and Gentlemen, Colonel Andrew Jackson and his wife, Mrs. Jackson." The band played a fanfare as Mr. Robinson dressed as Andrew Jackson entered. He led a woman in a pink satin ball gown down the stairs, her arm placed on his forearm.

No wonder he wanted us to attend; it gives him a chance to show off, CC thought. Mr. Robinson/Jackson stopped along the way and kissed hands as ladies curtseyed. He bowed to the men, some dressed in army uniforms. He recognized CC and walked over to her. "I'm so glad you could attend," he said. "This is my wife, Rachel." He introduced the woman to CC.

"It's nice to meet you, Mrs. Robertson."

Mr. Robertson/Jackson cleared his throat. "Ma'am, you're mistaken. This is my wife, Mrs. Rachel Jackson."

"So sorry, of course." CC curtseyed. "You have a beautiful home, Mrs. Jackson. Your costumes are so authentic."

"Ma'am, these aren't costumes. This is actually my formal dress uniform." Mr. Robertson/Jackson corrected her again.

CC thought she'd drink the Kool-Aid or, in this case, the punch. She would play her part and said, "I beg your pardon, Colonel Jackson. All this excitement has given me the vapors." She fanned herself with her ornate hand-painted fan.

"I'm sorry that Colonel Anderson won't be making an appearance tonight. His secretary informed me that he is not feeling well," Mr. Robertson/Jackson said.

"I'm sorry to hear that," CC said. "Maybe you can arrange for us to meet him at a later date."

The music started up and the dancing began before supper was announced. John Blackbear led Anne into the dining room. He held out her chair and then sat next to her. CC sat on the other side of Anne across from Mr. Robertson.

Liveried servants brought large silver platters bearing a variety of food, including roasted pheasant. After the main courses, the servants brought out a large cake known as an election cake. These cakes were made for large community gatherings.

After it was served, Mr. Robertson stood up and motioned to the band to stop playing. He tapped his glass and raised it. "To Nashville. To Tennessee. To the United States of America!"

"To Colonel Jackson!" someone across the table cried out.

The room filled with the clanking of glasses and cheers of "Huzzah."

Suddenly, the French doors burst open and two men in period costume burst into the room followed by a swirl of wind and rustling leaves. The flames in the chandeliers swayed and flickered. The first man was elegantly dressed; the second was garbed in the high collar and a black tie of a groomsman. He was carrying an ornate wooden box.

Mr. Robertson/Jackson stood up and exclaimed, "Dickinson, how dare you enter my home? What is the meaning of this?"

"You, sir, are a scoundrel and a coward! You reneged on our horse bet. I demand satisfaction!" said the Charles Dickinson impersonator.

"Sir, this is neither the place nor the time for your insults. I have guests. You embarrass yourself in front of my wife and our friends."

"Your wife is a bigamist."

"How dare you come into my home and insult my family!" Mr. Robertson/Jackson said, slamming his fist onto the table.

Dickinson motioned to his second, who placed the ornate wooden box on the dining room table in front of Mr. Robertson/Jackson. He unlocked it and opened it revealing two silver-handled dueling pistols. "I besiege you to examine the pistols. I challenge you to a duel at Harrison's Mill."

CC was all excited. She held up her fan to whisper to Anne, "You know, Anne, Andrew Jackson had a notorious temper and fought over a hundred duels. The man who broke in, Charles Dickinson, was one of his most famous duels. This will be exciting. Watch." She was enjoying the show. She knew the whole story of the May 30, 1806 conflict when Jackson and Dickinson fought a duel that ended poorly for Dickinson on the Red River in Kentucky.

The candles in the chandeliers flickered again; this time they were extinguished. The room went dark. Seconds later, there was a flash of light and then a gunshot. The guests screamed.

Someone turned on the auxiliary electric lights. CC and Anne were lying on the floor with Bradley on top of them. There was a gunshot hole in the back of the chair where CC's head could have been—should have been—if not for Bradley's quick thinking. "Bradley, what happened?" CC said. "How did you know?"

"I saw these men break into the house. I thought they might be trouble. By the time I came through the door, the candles went out. I could hear the cocking of the pistol, that's when I pushed you and Anne to safety," Bradley said.

Mr. Robertson/Jackson ran over to CC and helped her up. "Ms. Muller, the guns were not supposed to be loaded. This was to be a reenactment. I don't know what happened. I have no idea who fired the pistol."

He yelled for security. "Check the house. Check the grounds. Call the police!" The guests were still in shock and murmured in soft whispers amongst themselves.

CC looked on the table. The box was open with only one pistol remaining. The other one was missing. She examined the bullet hole in her chair. There was no possibility it was a misfire or an accident. Whoever had shot it was not only an expert marksman but could apparently see in the dark. She and Anne had been turning over stones and something evil had crawled out.

Later, Detective Clark, who had been the officer who questioned them after they had found Walters, arrived at the scene. Recognizing Anne and CC, he sighed and questioned them first, "Ms. Muller, Ms. Hillstrom, apparently all crimes in Nashville revolve around you. Can you tell me what happened?"

"Detective Clark, we were having a perfectly lovely dinner," Anne said, describing the feast. "We had pheasant, which was delicious. I usually don't care for gamey birds but this was perfectly done. For dessert, we had a delicious spiced election cake with fresh whipped cream. And a lovely raspberry cordial."

"And what about the gunshot?" he said with a deep sigh.

"Charles Dickinson's assistant set the dueling pistols on the table and opened the box. Then the candles blew out and the gun fired," CC said.

"Where is this assistant now?" Detective Clark looked around the room. The groups of elegantly clad guests were talking quietly as police officers gathered their information.

CC looked at Mr. Robertson. He shook his head. "I don't know. I don't know who he is. He wasn't the actor we used last year," he said. Mr. Robertson motioned for the Charles Dickinson impersonator to come over. "This is John Thompson, he's with the Historical Society. He played Charles Dickinson, my dueling adversary. John, this detective wants to speak to you."

"Where's the man who was helping you tonight?" Detective Clark asked.

"His name's Jenkins. I met him at the gun club. He's a regular there. When my usual assistant couldn't make it, I asked Jenkins if he could fill in," Johnson said.

While the detective was talking to Johnson, CC followed the trajectory line of the bullet hole from the back of her chair to the back wall. She found the ball lodged into the sideboard. She looked around to make sure no one saw her. Its bright sheen was not characteristic of an authentic lead ball that should have been used for the dueling pistol. It was a machined steel ball. She had been to the manufacturing plant and recognized it as coming from Southern Tradition Flintlocks. Upon closer examination, she saw their mark.

Detective Clark walked up to Anne and CC. "Once again, I'm asking you ladies to stay in town until we can wrap up all the investigations," he said.

John Blackbear walked Anne outside. "Anne, it's not safe for you here. I want you to come back to my house with me."

"John, I can't leave CC."

"CC is welcome also."

"I appreciate the offer but we have work to do. Antique hunting work. It's important work," Anne said.

John Blackbear bent down and kissed Anne. "The offer stands. You're always welcome at the reservation and in my home."

CC walked up to Anne after John Blackbear left. "So, what was that all about?"

"Nothing, it's been a long night. Let's go home."

Bradley opened the door of the Duesenberg and helped them into the back seat. He stuck his head in. "Are you sure you're both okay?"

Anne placed her gloved arm on Bradley's arm. "As long as you're around, I have a feeling we will always be okay, Bradley."

Chapter Twenty-nine

CC had just fallen asleep when she heard the message alert from her iPhone. It was on the nightstand next to her. Half asleep, she reached over, grabbed it and rubbed her eyes. It was from her friend at the *LA Times*. He gave her the name Jeremiah Riddle and a phone number. She turned off her phone and went back to sleep.

Later, Anne and CC sat in the Capital Bar and Grille, the elegant dark-wood restaurant located in the basement of the Hermitage hotel. CC was on her second cup of coffee. She loved their great French roast. Anne was still perusing the menu. She had to stop ordering pecan pancakes. It was all she had for breakfast since she had arrived in Tennessee but they were so good. She was starting to feel the consequences of the carb load, her pants were a little snug around the waist.

"Anne, the Tennessee 'Jack' Egg sandwich looks delicious. Why don't you give it a try?"

The waiter came over to take their order. "Can you tell me about this Tennessee egg sandwich?" Anne asked.

CC interrupted. "It's infused with Jack Daniel's whiskey."

The waiter smiled. "Yes, it's very popular with our guests."

"I've tried infusing my French toast with my homemade cherry wine. I'd love to learn how your chef prepares it."

"Oh, are you a chef?" the waiter asked.

"I dabble a bit," CC replied.

"I'm sure Chef Elbert would like to meet you. Would you like to come back to the kitchen?" the waiter asked.

She nodded and stood up. "I'll be right back," CC said to Anne before following the waiter into the kitchen. Anne rolled her eyes. Wearing his white toque, the chef was calling out orders and directing traffic in the busy kitchen.

"Chef Elbert, this is one of our guests, Ms. Muller. She's a chef. She wanted to watch you prepare the Tennessee Jack Egg sandwich," the waiter said, introducing CC to the world-famous chef.

"Of course." He nodded at her. CC watched as he infused the toast with Jack Daniels whiskey, fried an egg in a small pan with some bacon. When all the components were complete, he placed them artistically on the plate, garnishing the dish with house-made tomato gravy.

"Thank you so much, Chef Elbert. I can't wait to try that at home," CC said, marveling at the plate.

"The secret is to use jowl bacon," Chef Elbert said.

"I'm very familiar with jowl bacon. We had it often when I was growing up in Louisiana." CC paused. "Of course, one of my favorite breakfast recipes is for pain perdu; it's a New Orleans French toast."

"Please, I'd love to watch you make that." The Chef gestured at the oven and the pans.

CC took five eggs, half a cup of white sugar, and half a cup of milk. She fluttered around the kitchen until she found orange liqueur and added two tablespoons followed by a tablespoon of orange zest. She cut up a loaf of white bread into twelve slices. She combined the ingredients in a large bowl and beat them until they were thick and foamy. Then she poured the mixture into a shallow pan, she soaked the bread slices for two minutes on each side. She took a large griddle and turned on the heat to medium. She cooked the slices two minutes on each side until they were golden brown. She drizzled warm maple syrup on top and garnished it with a fresh orange slice. Chef Elbert tasted a slice. "Oh, Chef CC, this is delicious. I'd love to add this recipe to our Sunday brunch menu. We shall call it CC's French Toast."

CC smiled.

When CC returned to the table, Anne had already eaten half of her sandwich. The waiter brought CC the French toast. "That looks great, I didn't see that on the menu," Anne said.

"It's new." CC smiled.

After breakfast, CC went into one of the tiny rooms that served as a business center. She dialed Jeremiah Riddle's phone number. A woman answered, "Orange County Nursing Home. How may I help you?"

"I'm sorry. I was trying to reach Jeremiah Riddle. Is this the right number?"

"Oh, Jeremiah lives here. Please hold. I'll have the nurse let him know he has a phone call." A few seconds later, another female voice answered, "This is Nurse Nancy. I understand you want to speak with Mr. Riddle. Can I say who is calling?"

"He won't know me. My name is CC Muller. I'm calling about his brother."

The nurse handed the phone to Jeremiah Riddle. A very soft, southern raspy voice answered, "Hello."

"Mr. Riddle, my name is CC Muller. I wanted to ask you some questions about your brother, Clarence."

"Who are you?" he asked in a louder voice.

CC talked loudly into the phone. "We found some of your brother's sheet music and had some questions."

"I haven't seen my brother in 50 years. Not sure I can tell you anything."

"Do you know what happened to him?" CC asked, scribbling notes in her reporter's notebook.

"He left his kid on my doorstep and took off. Clarence was always irresponsible, drinking and rabble rousing."

"What happened to his child?"

"I raised him like he was my son. Who are you?" he asked in a confused voice.

"Is he still around?"

Mr. Riddle grew quiet for a moment. "CJ died years ago. He was too drunk to drive. He was an alcoholic like his father."

"I'm so sorry to hear this."

"Don't be sorry. He gave me a beautiful granddaughter, Lily. She took care of me when I got sick."

"Is she around? Can I talk to her?"

He dropped the phone. Nurse Nancy picked it up. "I'm sorry but you're upsetting Mr. Riddle," the nurse said.

"Is he okay?"

"He has advanced Alzheimer's."

"He seemed so lucid," CC said.

"You caught him on a good day," the nurse said.

"He mentioned his granddaughter. Do you know how I can get in touch with her?"

"She hasn't been around in months. He stopped recognizing her and when she would come visit him, he would get agitated," the nurse said.

"I'm so sorry. Do you know how I can reach her?"

"When I spoke to her last, she told me she was going to Nashville. She always had her guitar with her and played songs for Mr. Riddle," the nurse said. "We tried her number recently but it was disconnected."

"I'm in Nashville. I can try and find her," CC said. "Do you know what she looks like?"

The nurse hesitated. "I've got information about her biological grandfather. It's very important I get in touch with her," CC said.

"There's a picture of Mr. Riddle and his granddaughter next to his bed. I can make a copy and email it to you," the nurse said.

"Thank you. That would be great." CC gave the nurse her email address.

After hanging up the phone, CC turned a guilty look at the computer. It had been days since her last blog post. So many people were waiting, hanging on her every word. She opened up the site.

"Dear Friends, Please accept my apology for not writing more frequently. Anne and I have had quite an adventure that would rival anything Agatha Christie could dream up. The antique world holds so many dangers that we didn't foresee when we undertook our commission.

Through it all, Anne and I have remained true to the course. We have found many great items both for our client and for those of you on our list. We will be contacting you individually."

She detailed some of the stores they had visited and added pictures from her phone.

"The rest of the tale must be held back for now, due to police investigations. Enough said. But I promise you will know the whole story when the whole story is known. Until then, God bless all of you."

She posted the blog, and turned off the computer. When she opened the door of the business center, Bradley was standing at attention. She took a step back. "Bradley."

"Miss Muller, Miss Hillstrom wanted me to tell you that she is over at Betty's Boots on Broadway. I wanted to also give you fair warning that Betty's Boots caters to all the stars and their prices reflect it."

"Ohmiword," CC said, grabbing her purse.

"Will you be needing a ride?"

"Yes, Bradley."

By the time CC arrived at Betty's Boots, Anne was wearing a pair of light orchid Lucchese boots and a matching $3,000 lambskin fringed skirt. A sequined cowboy hat completed the outfit.

CC sighed. "Anne, we can't afford any of it."

The salesgirl frowned. "We have layaway."

Anne turned to CC. "Layaway. Layaway." She admired herself in the mirror, twirling so the fringe swirled around her. "CC, we'll be getting that big commission check from Betsy."

"Anne, do you have any idea what the Hermitage is costing daily? If you really want the boots, we can stay at a different hotel and save money," CC said.

Anne's face turned white. She turned to the salesgirl. "I will not be purchasing these items today."

"Anne, we have to go. I have a lead on Riddle."

With one last glance at the full-length mirror, Anne reluctantly changed back to her street clothes. "You sure you don't want to do layaway?" the salesgirl asked, taking the boots and skirt from her.

Pausing for a moment, Anne shook her head no. She followed CC out of the store and into the street where one drunken tourist was practicing a line dance in the middle of the street while other tourists cheered her on. Anne wanted to join in. CC pulled her arm and led her to the black Lincoln town car before she could ask.

Chapter Thirty

CC knocked on Brent's door. Anne sat in the town car, looking up her bank balance. She clicked on her calculator on her iPhone, subtracted her mortgage, her utility bills from her check and then compared that to the price of Betty's Boots and realized she could live in her house for the next six months or get the outfit. It was a tough decision.

CC waved to Anne to come in as Brent opened the door. "Miss Hillstrom, do you want me to wait for you?" Bradley asked.

"We're going to need the Volkswagen."

"I'll have someone drop it off for you. "

"Bradley, you're wonderful. Could you have someone pack a lunch, too?"

"Certainly, Miss Hillstrom." Bradley disappeared with the Lincoln town car. The Hermitage was a pretty penny but worth every cent. The blog request list was paying the bill along with Betsy's commission. Anne felt it was a good business investment. After all, the Hermitage was a good place to network with wealthy collectors who might want to hire the Spoon Sisters.

Anne and CC sat on the couch across from Brent. It was nearly lunchtime and Brent was just waking up. Part of a musician's life. He was wearing cargo shorts, sandals and no shirt. His 30-year-old body was slender but cut. He pulled his hair back into a topknot and wrapped a rubber band around it. He sipped his coffee from his Gruhn vintage guitar coffee cup.

"Brent, we didn't wake you, did we?" CC asked.

"No, I've been up for minutes." He smiled.

"Lots of things have happened since I saw you last."

"A lot of things happened when I last saw you."

CC blushed.

Brent sipped his coffee and smiled again.

Anne was not following the conversation.

"I need your help with something." CC pulled up the photos on her iPhone. "I received this picture of Lily Riddle. She's a singer/songwriter. I was hoping you might know her."

Brent took the iPhone, looked at Lily's picture. "I've seen her around town. I didn't know her name. She's very good."

CC took back her phone. "Any idea where I could find her?"

"There's a listing service for all the bars. It's in the *Nashville Entertainer*. Also, you might want to try Music Row if she's trying to break in. She's probably playing on the street like everyone else. Last time I saw her she was in line at the Bluebird for open mic night. I don't remember her playing. She probably didn't make it in."

"Brent, can you ask some of your friends? If they've seen her? It's really important that I get in touch with her," CC said.

"Is this about the recording of 'Young Hearts'?"

"Yeah, she's Clarence Riddle's granddaughter. Everything goes back to Clarence Riddle. I need to talk to her."

Brent put his coffee down, stretched and yawned. "I'll ask around town. Maybe you can stop by later tonight and I'll have some information. I'm playing the Listening Room Café if you want to stop in. The food's pretty good. I know the music's good." He gave her a wink.

CC smiled. Anne still wasn't following the conversation. There was a knock on the door. It was one of the valets was dropping off the keys to the VW. CC took the keys and turned to Brent. "We'll see you later," she said.

Anne followed her out the door toward the VW. "What was that flirting all about?"

"I wasn't flirting. I wanted to see if he could help us find Lily." They got in the VW. Anne was distracted by the wicker basket sitting on her seat. She took a peek inside and caught a whiff of balsamic vinaigrette. She opened one of the containers. It was sirloin tip salad with fresh vegetables and goat cheese. A warm baguette was accompanying it with a container of apple butter and sparkling water. Anne nibbled on a piece of sirloin tip, hoping CC wouldn't notice.

"Anne, can you wait til we pull over? I'd like to eat, too."

Anne looked over with the piece of steak hanging out of her mouth and nodded.

When she stopped the car so they could eat, CC said, "You know, Anne, the chef at the Hermitage runs his own farm with all his own grass-fed cattle. It's the true farm to table."

They sat at a picnic table at a nice park and enjoyed their lunch *al fresco*. "I've got a lead for us. There's a woman in Franklin. Her husband was a contractor and worked on a lot of the local bars and recording studios. He's got a three-car garage full of stuff."

"Sounds great," Anne said, finishing her last bite of the famous Hermitage Hotel coconut cake. She then proceeded to lick her fork. She paused, licked the fork again. She then looked over lovingly at CC's fork that still had a big chunk of frosting on it but thought better of asking.

Chapter Thirty-one

Anne and CC got back in the VW and headed towards Franklin. It was a small suburb of Nashville. The urban landscape turned into farmettes and then into gravel back roads until they reached a small, two-bedroom, aluminum-sided house.

Its owner, Marsha Casper, walked down the stairs to greet them. "It's so nice to meet you," Marsha said. "Thank you for driving out here. We're back in the woods here as you can tell. I'm glad you could find it."

"Thank you for having us. We're excited about looking at the garage," CC said.

"Let me take you over." She walked over to the large, oversized garage, located behind the house and lifted one of the three doors. "As I told you on the phone, my husband Bob passed a few years ago."

"I'm so sorry."

"Thank you. He didn't throw anything out. Any worksite he was on if someone didn't want it, it was his. Nothing's organized. Be careful."

"Oh, we're antique hunters. We know our way around clutter." Anne pictured her living room.

The first thing that caught CC's eye was an old leather swivel barstool. "This looks pretty old. Like 1960s."

"Hold on," Marsha said. "Kind of a funny story. Bob was fixing the refrigeration unit at the Dewdrop Inn in Murfreesboro and Merle Haggard came in for a beer. He wound up on that stool all night drinking. Bob matched him beer for beer. Merle became a regular at that bar, always sitting on that stool. Eventually, Bob was able to talk Merle into autographing it. The bar owner gave it to Bob as payment. There's a picture inside the house of Merle sitting on the stool. The only thing left of the bar is the stool."

CC looked at Anne with a big smile. "Let's put this in our pile." The next thing CC saw was a pink nose sticking out from underneath some pieces of wood. She moved the wood away and nearly jumped back. It was a stuffed possum. She picked it up, examined it and saw George Jones' signature. "I have to ask. Where did Bob get the possum?"

"That's another funny story." Marsha smiled at the memory. "Bob was on a fishing trip on Old Hickory when him and his buddies stopped at the taxidermy. He wanted to have his bass mounted. He walked in and George Jones was picking up a fish he had mounted. Bob got to talking. Bob was really good at talking. He told George that he was a big fan. The taxidermist had this possum and Bob bought it from him. Bob asked George—you know George's nickname is the possum––to sign it. Bob named the possum George. He used to be on our mantle but I moved him out to the garage. He scared me in the middle of the night when I went for my midnight snack."

"This goes in the pile." CC moved the possum to the corner where she had placed the barstool. CC poked through a cardboard box, which held picture frames, baseball cards and old tools. She found a trucker cap with the Texas flag on the bill. CC held it up. "What's with the hat?"

"Look around back," Marsha said.

CC turned it around. It was signed by Willie Nelson.

"Bob was working at West End Studios in Nashville. He was putting in a bathroom and Willie Nelson was recording. They got to talking as he would do. Willie liked Bob's hat. It said Bob's Construction. Willie said he would trade hats with him. I got a picture of Willie wearing that exact hat at Farm Aid."

CC looked at Anne. "I can't stop."

Peeking in the corner, Anne removed a sheet that was covering a large farm table. On the table were old Mammy cookie jars, salt and pepper shakers and a large sign.

"Oh, dear, I never liked those much. They were my grandmother's," Marsha said, shuddering. "I couldn't throw them out. I keep them out here in the garage."

"I've got someone on my list," Anne said, pulling the notebook from her large orange Prada bag. She skimmed through it and found Professor Frank Barton from the University of Alabama. He's writing a book about the way *mammy* was depicted throughout the years. These would be perfect for his collection. "Would you be willing to part with these?"

Marsha paused for a moment. "They were my grandmother's. Even though I don't care for them, they *are* part of my family history."

"It's got a lot of historical value that my client, a professor, will pass on to his students. He teaches African American studies. How long have these been under that sheet out here?"

Marsha thought. "At least 20 years. We moved them out of the house when my kids were little."

"Don't you think it's better they're rescued and given a good home? You know my great aunt Sybil once called beautiful pieces like this *orphaned artifacts*. Left to their own, they would never have a family. We can give them a family now."

"That sounds good. You can take them."

"Did Bob do a lot of work at West End?" CC asked.

"He was over there all the time. He fixed their air conditioning, heating. Something was always breaking down there. The guy who owned it never seemed to have enough money to fix it right so he always had Bob patching stuff up. Bob never minded though. He liked meeting all the musicians. In fact, I've got some photographs of him with a lot of them. Follow me into the house." Marsha led the way into the living room. One entire wall was covered with framed photos.

CC recognized one as Clarence Riddle sitting with his Martin guitar in front of a microphone at the studio––in the sound booth. She could make out Colonel Anderson and Walters, the engineer.

"Anne, look at this. Hopkins told us that Walters left Colonel Anderson to start West End Studios because he was angry with him. Here he is with the Colonel recording Clarence Riddle." CC removed the picture from the wall and stared at it. "Can I buy this photo?"

Marsha nodded her agreement. "You can have this one. I've got so many."

They sat down at her kitchen table and she poured glasses of sweet tea. She brought over a bowl of fresh honey. Anne took a spoonful. "This is delicious honey. Where'd you get this from?"

"Oh, I keep bees. It's been a really bad year. I've lost a lot of bees. Something is killing them. I can't figure it out. I used to sell the honey at the farmer's market, but I don't have enough this year. That's part of the reason I'm selling off Bob's stuff."

As she spoke, CC noticed the burn mark on Marsha's right hand. It was blistering. "Have you been in the garden today?"

"I was out there this morning, cleaning up some of the leaves."

"Do you mind if I take a look? I'm a gardener too." CC followed Marsha out to the garden. She examined the ground around the hives. She pushed some leaves around. Then she took out a napkin and wrapped something up. Marsha watched intensely. While CC was conducting her investigation, Anne was watching several items on eBay, including a blue multicolored Victorian-era Longwy candlestick. A steal at only $19.99.

They sat back at the kitchen table. CC placed the napkin on the table and unfolded it carefully, revealing a black bug. "Here's your culprit," CC said.

"What is it?"

"It's called an American oil beetle. This is what's been killing your bees."

"Not bees again," Anne moaned.

"What do you mean?" Marsha asked.

"We had a little trouble with bees about a year ago. It's a long story but it involved honey bee pheromone."

CC ignored her and kept talking, "American oil beetles are a type of blister beetle. When threatened, they emit a chemical called cantharidin that creates blisters and irritates human skin. I noticed the blisters on your hand. You must have brushed up against one in the garden. They're usually more active in the spring, but I noticed one or two are still out there."

"Do they eat my bees?"

"These beetles don't fly. They're really slow. The larvae are very devious. They sit on flowers waiting for a bee to land, then they latch onto the bee for a free ride to the hive. Once there, the beetle larvae feed on the bee larvae," CC explained.

"I can't believe that. It's the first year I've ever had problems. What do I do about it?"

"First thing you can do is pick the beetles off your plants. Make sure you wear gloves. Next, leave a wide row between plantings and clear out the surrounding weeds. Blister beetles do not cross wide rows and they do not like to enter empty spaces. Here's what I've found to be really effective, take some horseradish root, mix it in water and spray all your plants. It won't harm your bees, but it will take care of your blister beetle problem."

"How can I ever thank you?"

"No thanks are necessary. If you have any more questions, read my blog. I give gardening tips every week."

Anne retrieved an antique hunters' business card. "Here's the URL for the blog. We'd love to have you as a fan."

"I'm a fan already," Marsha said, holding the card.

As she opened the front door to leave, CC paused. Sitting in the glass oak display case next to the couch was a 1942 German Luger. "Can I see that?" CC asked.

Marsha unlocked the case and brought the pistol out. She handed it to CC.

CC held it in her hand, admiring the ivory grips. It had an officer's initials engraved on it in German, and the barrel was inlaid with semi-precious jewels. "This is beautiful. Do you know the story behind it?"

"Bob's grandfather took it from a German officer he captured. The officer surrendered himself in Commerce, France. Bob's grandfather was a private. He kept it as a souvenir and gave it to Bob."

"It's beautiful German craftsmanship," CC said.

Anne watched. The pistol was pushing all CC's buttons—German precision and steel. The only part Anne admired were the jewels. "Growing up in Germany, I shot a similar Luger. It was my grandfather's," CC said. "He was actually in the resistance in the Black Forest fighting the Nazis. He taught me how to shoot. I would love to shoot this gun. Would you consider selling it?"

"CC, you know that one of our clients collects military memorabilia and weapons. This hits both," Anne interrupted.

CC gave Anne a stern look but then her practical side took over. "Marsha, would you consider parting with it? It will go to a good home. Our client is a decorated war veteran. I think he'd be excited to add it to his collection."

Marsha eyed the gun and CC. "Bob would want it to go to a good home."

"We need to bring it to a gun dealer so you can sign it over to me," CC said after they settled on a price.

"There's a gun range that Bob used ten minutes down the road if you want to go now. You can shoot it there too," Marsha said.

CC's face lit up. It was the best of both worlds. She would be able to shoot this German officer's gun and fulfill one of her client's wishes.

After the girls loaded the VW microbus with their finds from Marsha's garage, they drove the short distance to the Franklin gun range, following Marsha at a safe pace. The gun range was located on the site of a former Civil War armory. The building still looked as if it could hold several Rebel cannons. The iron door opened with little resistance. Inside, the walls were lined with hunting rifles, paramilitary assault guns and several glass cases filled with handguns. It was not an unfamiliar sight to CC who appreciated any finely tuned machine.

Anne hung back, looking at the hats and the selection of beef jerky.

"May I help you, ladies?" asked a 50-ish woman with long bleached blonde hair. She was wearing a T-shirt that read *Franklin Guns*. Strapped to her belt was a pearl-handled stainless steel Kimber .45 automatic. Her name tag read *Blanche*.

Marsha placed the case with the Luger inside on the counter and opened it. Blanche smiled. "That's quite a fancy Luger."

"We'd like to transfer the ownership, and I'd like to shoot it first to make sure it's in good working condition," CC said.

"There's a $10 fee for an instant background check, and we need to take your fingerprints. Are you from Tennessee?" Blanche handed her several forms.

"I'm from Illinois. I do have a conceal carry license, and I have a FBI profile from my years as an investigative reporter. I've worked with the FBI as an expert consultant."

"When was that?" Anne said, over her shoulder.

CC ignored her.

"All I need is $10 and your fingerprints," Blanche said.

As CC knew it would, her background check came back perfect. She bought a box of 9-millimeter bullets. Blanche gave her earphones and a target. The indoor gun range was empty except for one shooter in a stall. CC clipped the bull's eye target onto the pulley. She pushed the button and the target flew down the range. She stopped at 25 feet, thought about it and pushed it again. She stopped it at 50 feet. She loaded the clip. It slid in and engaged smoothly like she knew it would. Bob had taken great care of it. She could smell the oil and the grease. She aimed, held her breath and gently squeezed the trigger. The trigger pulled with little effort. After six shots, she had a perfect quarter-sized grouping around the bull's eye. She finished the 50 rounds and then returned to the front.

"So, how'd you like it?" Blanche asked.

CC pulled her earphones off and smiled. "It's great." She looked over at Anne who shook her head no.

The girls loaded up their car and headed back to the Hermitage. Clutching her small mason jar of honey, Anne thought about calling Bradley on the way to prepare her bath. But she didn't want CC to hear her.

She would have to wait.

Chapter Thirty-two

Soaking in the bubbles, Anne relaxed and read through the room service menu. She clicked on the 20-inch LED TV that hung over the bathtub and flipped through the channels to watch the weather report. The perky weather girl was predicting more rain and flood warnings. Anne then flipped on the shopping channels. There was nothing on either shopping channel so she went back to the news. Behind the newscaster was the image of Andrew Jackson's Hermitage Plantation. She turned the volume up.

"Police have arrested a man of interest regarding the shooting at the historical society's recent ball at the Hermitage Plantation." Behind the newscaster, a small graphic showed a mug shot of the suspect. "A Nashville resident, his name is Ricky Jenkins."

"CC get in here quick!" Anne called.

The bathroom door opened. "What?" CC asked, as she walked in with her eyes covered.

"Look at the TV. They caught the shooter from the plantation."

CC gave a quick look at the screen, her hand on the doorknob. Then she looked again. Ricky Jenkins had a blue note tattoo on his neck.

The newscast showed the exterior of the plantation and then the dining room. In the background of the dining room video, CC and Anne could be seen sitting at the table, talking to the police officers. "Look! There we are!" Anne pointed a soapy hand at the screen.

Chapter Thirty-three

Brent was waiting outside the front door of the Listening Room Café. He waved at Anne and CC as they walked up to the entrance. "I told Lily you were coming. She's waiting in the green room." Brent nodded at the hostess as he led CC and Anne into the crowded place. Tables and chairs were lined up facing the stage. They walked past all that and to a small room behind the stage.

A little five foot tall woman with long blonde hair sat tuning her Martin guitar. She couldn't be more than nineteen years old. She looked up; her green eyes sparkling like emeralds. CC could see the resemblance to her grandfather. She was a beautiful young woman. Her eyes, though they sparkled, held a lot of sadness. She was wearing torn jeans, cowboy boots and a long-sleeve black shirt.

Brent stuck his head in. "Lily, this is Anne and CC."

CC smiled, walked over and held out her hand.

Ignoring CC's hand, Lily continued tuning the guitar, her ear bent close to the strings.

"Lily, do you think we could have a couple minutes of your time?" CC asked.

Lily looked up at them. "Brent got me a gig opening for him tonight in exchange for talking with you, so you got a minute." She looked at them again. "You look familiar. Do I know you?"

"We were just on TV, on the news," Anne said. "We were at the Hermitage plantation. There was an incident."

"Oh, yeah, I saw that."

"We have some questions about your grandfather," CC said.

Lily stopped tuning and looked up. "My grandfather's in a nursing home in California."

CC continued. "I meant your biological grandfather. Clarence Riddle."

Lily put the guitar in its case. "I can't help you with that. I never met him."

CC sat down on the small tattered couch next to Lily. "We found a tape of his and some sheet music. I thought you might want to see it."

"Why would I want to do that?"

"Your grandfather was a very talented songwriter, singer and from what I found out, he wrote a lot of hit songs. He never got credit for them. I think if you just look at this sheet music you'd have a better idea of who he was."

While CC was talking, Anne pulled the sheet music out of her bag and handed it to Lily. Lily picked up her Martin, leaned the sheet music against the case and started playing. She stopped about halfway through and wiped her eyes. Then she continued playing again. When she was done, she sat and stared at the music. It was like looking at her grandfather's face. She knew in three and a half minutes who he was, and what was in his heart. The notes on the lines were like words whispered in her head. She felt a connection.

Anne pulled a handkerchief out of her bag and handed it to Lily who waved her away. "It's a nice song."

"We have a friend who's connected in Nashville. He knows a lot of important people in the music world. I think the whole story of Clarence Riddle and his granddaughter would be compelling," CC said.

"I have my own songs. That's why I'm here. It took

me a year to get a chance to play on this stage for fifteen minutes. I've had a lot of doors shut on me." She handed the sheet music back to Anne and stood up holding her guitar. "My grandfather abandoned my father and then my father abandoned me. I don't want anything to do with his music. I have to go on stage."

Walking back to the front of the café, Brent led Anne and CC over to a small table in the corner. He ordered a pitcher of beer. "Brent, thanks for finding her for us," CC said.

"I'm sorry it didn't work out," he said, sitting on one of the barstools. "I think she's really talented. I'd like to see her get a break."

CC took out her iPhone and recorded Lily's set. She was amazing. She could hear the heartbreak in her voice. She could tell that she lived these songs. When she was done, CC whispered to Anne. "We have to show this to Steven."

Chapter Thirty-four

Anne and CC arrived early morning at Kendall Enterprises. Anne's stomach growled. They hadn't had time to stop at the Pancake Pantry. CC was afraid the line was too long.

When they arrived at his office, Steven came out to greet them. "I'm glad to see you. I just got off the phone with Betsy. Please come in my office." They followed him. "Can I get you some coffee?"

Anne eyed the box of Gigi's cupcakes sitting next to the coffeemaker. She wondered what flavors were inside. She was on vacation sort of, so she was off her diet. One cupcake would be okay. She took one finger and slightly lifted the lid, bending down to take a peek inside.

"Anne," CC blurted.

Anne closed the lid and went back into Steven's office. They sat down on the couch across from Steven.

"We wanted to talk to you about this amazing singer we saw last night." CC played a short clip of Lily's set from her iPhone.

"She's very good, but I don't usually deal with the talent. I have staff that know that area better than I do," Steven said.

"It's an interesting story. When Anne and I were looking for antiques for the coach house, we discovered this sheet music that was a lost song written by Clarence Riddle. You must have heard the name, Clarence Riddle?" CC asked.

"That name has been around Nashville," Steven said,

looking down at his iPhone.

"We tracked down his granddaughter who's a musician. That's the girl on the recording—Lily Riddle. What a great story it would be to have her playing her grandfather's music. A struggling young street musician carrying on the family tradition."

Anne interrupted, "She also writes her own songs. They're really good. Those are the ones she's playing on the video."

"Do you have that Clarence Riddle song?" Steven asked.

"We have it locked up in the safe in our hotel room."

"I'd be interested in seeing it. It could be an interesting story," Steven said. He opened his desk drawer and pulled out a business card. He scribbled on the back of it. "Give this to her. It's John Lloyd's number. He's a producer at Dog Ear Music, one of my subsidiaries. It's on Music Row. I'll let him know she's coming. If he likes her, we can help her out."

CC took the card and slid it in to her purse.

"How's the antique hunting going?" Steven asked as he walked them to the door.

"I think you will be very pleased." CC shook Steven's hand. Anne grabbed a cupcake and followed CC out the door.

Chapter Thirty-five

Anne and CC sat in the Nashville police station waiting for Detective Clark. He was not eager to see the two tourists. He made them sit for two hours. While they waited, Anne browsed her eBay watch lists on her cell phone. When Clark finally came out to them, CC stood up.

"Come back to my desk," Detective Clark said. They followed him through the corridor to a crowded room full of desks. He sat down behind one and opened a manila file folder. Anne and CC sat across from him. "What brings you in now?"

"We saw that you brought Ricky Jenkins in to question him about the shooting at the party. We wanted to see if we could be of any help," CC said, sitting forward on the uncomfortable wooden chair.

"You stated you didn't see the shooter so what help can you be? Do you know Mr. Jenkins?" Detective Clark sat back on his wooden office chair so it was balanced on the back two legs.

"No, but I can verify that he was in the room, and that he is left-handed," CC said. "When he placed the heavy pistol box on the table, I noticed he balanced the weight with his left hand. And the angle of the bullet hole in the back of my chair and the height of the table from where it was fired indicates the trajectory was from a left-handed shooter."

Detective Clark just stared at her. "Yes, he is left-handed and he's admitted he shot the pistol. According to Jenkins, however; it was an accident. He was removing the pistol from the box. The gentlemen were going to reenact the Dickinson/Jackson duel outside. Mr. Robertson was to examine the pistol according to dueling protocol. Jenkins had left the door open, and a wind blew out the candles as he was handing the pistol to Robertson when the gun misfired. That's his story."

"And he just happened to be pointing it at my head?" CC asked.

"You were sitting across from the pistol box. Just bad luck," Detective Clark said, sitting forward in his chair. "Is there any reason why Mr. Jenkins would want to harm you? You said you've never met him before."

"We've never met before but I recognized his tattoo. The man who attacked us in the alley had a tattoo on his neck."

"Was it the same tattoo?"

"I couldn't see it clearly. It was dark and he was covered in blood," CC said.

"According to the report, you never saw the attacker's face. Is that correct?"

"Yes." CC paused and asked. "Who was responsible for loading the pistols?"

Detective Clark was starting to get frustrated. "We're looking into it. The pistols belong to the Historical Society's collection. The members frequently shoot them at the range. According to Jenkins, he didn't load them. We don't know yet who loaded the pistols. Jenkins voluntarily came into the station to explain what happened."

"I'd like to talk to him," CC said.

"For now, he's not here. We questioned him and released him," Detective Clark said.

"Thank you," CC said.

Detective Clark walked them back to the front door. Anne and CC stepped out into the bright late afternoon sunshine. "What do we do now?' Anne asked.

"We go to Ricky Jenkins' house," CC said.

"We don't know where he lives."

"Yes, we do. I read his file which was on the detective's desk." After years as a reporter, CC had honed her skills to read upside down. She had made out the address and memorized it. She put the address in her GPS.

Chapter Thirty-six

The apartment complex on the west end of Nashville was located in the middle of what appeared to be housing projects. At this point, it was eight o'clock and already dark. "Do you think this is a good idea? Could we wait til tomorrow during the day?" Anne said.

"We're here now."

"Do you think he's going to confess to attempted murder? Is that why we're here?" Anne asked, glancing around nervously.

"Anne, I've interviewed enough criminals throughout the years to know when they're lying."

Does the steel industry harbor a lot of criminals? Anne wondered. It might be time to read one of CC's steel industry articles. Maybe there was more going on than she thought.

CC continued, "I want to look him in the eye and see if he's lying." She turned off the car in front of the two-story apartment complex. She gathered up her courage. Weeds filled the front yard. Out in front was a broken down rusty pickup truck. The rain started again.

Good, Anne thought, *fewer people out and about.* She followed CC to the front porch. CC took her finger and ran it down the list of apartment doorbells til she came to the name *Jenkins*. She buzzed and took a deep breath. She waited a minute and buzzed it again.

"I don't think he's home. Let's go," Anne said, looking over her shoulder. She had an uneasy feeling like she was being watched.

As they were waiting, an old man opened the door

and stumbled out. CC smelled the liquor on him. He gave them a wild-eyed look and brushed past them. CC grabbed the door before it closed. They walked up the stairs to the second floor, to apartment 223. CC knocked. Still no answer.

"That's it. We tried everything we could. Let's go." Anne clutched her large orange Prada bag. It, and she, were not accustomed to this environment.

CC reached into her small white Coach purse and retrieved one of the items she never traveled without, her Diebolt professional lock picking kit. She only used it when absolutely necessary. This seemed to be one of those occasions.

"You've got to be kidding me! Breaking and entering?" Anne said.

CC started to pick the lock and the door swung open. She turned to Anne. "Entering, not breaking." The small studio apartment was empty except for beer cans and garbage on the floor, a couple of folding chairs and a couch.

"Looks like he left in a hurry," Anne said, thinking maybe they should too. She looked over her shoulder again. "I feel like we're being watched," Anne whispered to CC.

"Don't be ridiculous," CC said, walking around the room. In the corner were colored light gels, surge protectors, cables, wire crimpers, LED lights and strobe lights.

As CC was looking, Anne went over to the window. The shade was down and filthy. She reached into her large bag and pulled out her evening gloves.

"What are you doing?" CC asked.

"I'm the lookout. I'm keeping watch for Jenkins." The lone streetlight flickered. In the rain, she could make out a large figure skulking in the shadows. Then it was gone. "CC, I think someone is out there."

"Is it Jenkins? Is he coming this way?" CC looked up from where she had dumped one of the large contractor black garbage bags.

"No, I think he saw me looking out the window and he took off," Anne said before peeking out the window again. She could see red tail lights disappearing into the night.

CC reached into her purse again and pulled out a pair of surgical gloves and put them on. She took a pencil and carefully began lifting up the garbage. She waded through old Chinese food and rotting takeout containers. "What are you looking for?" Anne whispered.

"I don't think Mr. Jenkins is very bright." CC said, as she found what she was looking for. Soaked in sweet and sour sauce was a receipt from Southern Tradition Flintlocks for black powder and steel balls. Then something else caught her eye. Underneath a box of rotten fried rice, she found a Dave Southwell road crew ID. She gingerly picked it up with the pencil and hung it in the air for Anne to see. "Jenkins was Southwell's lighting engineer. I think he killed Southwell." CC put both items in a baggie and then into her purse. "That's why he's been after us. He wants those photos of the lighting rigging I took. Let's get out of here, Anne."

CC led the way out the door and back to the VW. Anne watched over her shoulder as they exited the building. She couldn't shake the uneasy feeling of being watched. They got in the VW and headed back to the Hermitage Hotel. "When I was looking at Jenkins' police file, it said that his attorney, a Clifford Holmes came in with him," CC said.

"And?"

"And," CC continued, "I Googled his law firm. He's a partner in one of the largest law firms in Tennessee."

"Why would a big shot attorney be interested in

Jenkins? Did you see his apartment? I don't think he has a lot of money," Anne said.

"Somebody didn't want Jenkins to talk."

Chapter Thirty-seven

Dog Ear Records' offices were located down the street from Kendall Enterprises in a large stainless steel office building. The smooth polished exterior reflected their images as Anne and CC walked up to the front door. Anne paused to admire her new cowboy boots. Not the $1,000 Lucchese ones, but the more reasonably priced $300 Dan Posts in turquoise with red roses.

CC stopped and touched the side of the building. She was about to explain to Anne where the steel came from when the security guard opened the front double-glass doors. "Hi, I'm CC Muller. We're here to see John Lloyd. We're friends of Steven Kendall's."

The guard held the door open and let them in. "Please sign in and have a seat." The lobby was quiet. Artist photos hung on the wall, including a recent one of Dave Southwell. Anne nudged CC and pointed out the picture. They sat in the uncomfortably modern white and steel chairs. "You know this doesn't feel much like a creative space, does it?" Anne commented.

After a few minutes, Anne walked over to the guard who was now sitting at the entry desk. As she and CC waited, she had heard him coughing. "Are you okay? Do you need a cough drop?" She went to reach into her large orange Prada bag.

"I'm fine." He waved her off, taking a large sip of his coffee. "Allergies," he said. His nametag read, *Jeffrey*. He was stout, in his late 60s, and his little white goatee jiggled when he talked. Anne was reminded of a Billy goat.

"What are you allergic to?" Anne asked.

"What aren't I allergic to? Mostly mold and mildew."

Anne looked around the pristine stainless steel and glass lobby. She glanced back at Jeffrey, the security guard, and noticed his 60-ounce coffee mug, which read "World's Greatest Grandpa." "That's quite a coffee mug you have there," Anne said.

"I fill it two or three times a day. I've got to have my caffeine," Jeffrey said.

"I'm the same way," CC said. "I make fresh pressed coffee every morning."

Anne ignored the conversation. She examined his workstation. Behind him, was a stainless steel counter with a large pod coffeemaker and a carousel holding pods.

"Must take a lot of pods to fill that up," Anne said.

Behind her, CC hovered, skimming the company's website from her iPhone.

Jeffrey sipped his coffee, not looking up from the monitor screen embedded in his desktop.

Anne walked behind him and studied the coffeemaker. "Jeffrey, how do you like this coffeemaker? I don't have one. I have an old percolator. I like the sound it makes but this seems more convenient."

He didn't answer. Anne continued to study the coffeemaker as Jeffrey collapsed into a coughing fit. She eyed him with concern. After he was done coughing, she asked, "Jeffrey, how often do you clean this?"

"I never clean it." He cleared his throat. "I have to fill the water reservoir after three or four cups of coffee so it's always fresh water." He swallowed some more coffee.

Anne removed the reservoir and took the back cover off the two-channel feeder. She pulled the tube out and showed it to Jeffrey. "As I expected, Jeffrey, even though the water is constantly replenished, the coffeemaker only heats up to 130 degrees. It's not hot enough to kill the bacteria. Water remains in the feeder tube. Mold heats up enough to cause an enzyme reaction when combined with your Colombian coffee grounds. It emulsifies, releasing the mold into your coffee. That's what's irritating your airways."

Jeffrey put his coffee down mid-sip and slid it across the counter like it was poisoned. He swiveled his chair around to face Anne. He gave her a Billy goat smile.

"If you run a ten percent vinegar solution through it once a week, it should be fine." She reached into her large bag, pulled out a small vial and handed it to him.

"What's this?" he asked.

"This is butterbur." At his confused look, Anne explained, "It's an herb that works as a leukotriene inhibitor. It blocks the chemicals that trigger swelling in the nasal passage. It's natural and won't make you sleepy like prescription antihistamine. I've spent a lot of time researching non-pharmaceutical natural treatments. I find this works best."

"Thanks . . ." Jeffrey stared at the small vial.

"Anne Hillstrom," she finished for him and shook his hand. "Have you worked here long?"

"Been here since the doors opened. I came over from our previous location and oversaw the security installation in this building." Jeffrey paused. "I began with the company when I returned home from Vietnam in 1968. Now I'm semi-retired. Those were the days." He stopped, reminiscing.

"Go on," Anne encouraged him.

"In the beginning, it was me, Larry Walters and the

Colonel. That's when we were still called Blue Note Records. We had a small storefront on the west end of the city." He pointed to a black and white picture over his head that showed a single-story square building with a hand-scrawled *Blue Note Records* on the picture window.

Anne and CC both stared at the picture. They had been there and they had met Walters.

"Blue note?" CC asked.

Jeffrey rolled up a sleeve of his white cotton button down and showed them a blue note tattoo. "Yeah, we all got these when the company was incorporated. It was the Colonel's idea."

"Who else got the tattoo?"

"All of us. To start, the Colonel, me, Walters. As Blue Note grew, other staff who the Colonel trusted and mentored would show their loyalty by getting the tattoo." Jeffrey pointed again to the picture behind him. "When we left the original building to move here, the Colonel changed the name to Dog Ear Records after his basset hound. Walters bought the old building and started West End Studios. When the Colonel retired, the company was never the same. It wasn't family anymore. It was just a job."

Anne's phone vibrated. She reached into her bag. When she pulled it out, she saw the icon with the Union Jack. It was Nigel. She put the phone up to her ear and walked toward the front door. "Nigel, is that you? I have bad reception. Let me step outside." She walked out of the building and stood by the front door, once again admiring the reflection of her new boots in the shiny steel.

"Anne," the British voice replied. "I emailed you a copy of the coroner's report. It was determined that Walters drowned. He had an epileptic seizure that lasted about 30 minutes and fell face first into a puddle."

"Thank you, Nigel, I'll look at the report."

"Oh, Anne, when you're back in town. . . " Nigel's voice continued as Anne clicked off the phone.

CC came out the door. "Who was that?"

"That was Nigel. Walters died from drowning during an epileptic seizure." Anne hesitated and then repeated, "Seizure." She pulled a brown prescription bottle out of her large purse and tried to make out the label.

"What's that?" CC asked.

"I found this at West End Studios. It says *Walters*. It appears to be felbamate." Anne paused. "It's used to control epileptic seizures. I've tested similar medications. This one's used when no other medications are effective. He must have had severe epilepsy." She opened the bottle, took out the last remaining pill and sniffed it. Then she gave it a lick. "Tastes sweet. That's not right. I need to analyze this."

"Anne, we don't have access to a lab," CC said.

She hit the speed dial on her phone. Bradley answered. "Oh, Miss Hillstrom, how may I help you?"

"Bradley, this may sound like a strange request. Do you have access to an ion spectrometer?" she asked.

"Why, certainly, Miss. Hillstrom. I have a friend at Vanderbilt. Let me call him."

"You know, Anne, ion spectrometry is also used to detect chemical warfare," CC said.

"Yes, CC, I know."

Chapter Thirty-eight

The black Lincoln town car pulled up in front of the science building at Vanderbilt University. The area was crowded with young medical students wearing white lab coats walking briskly. Bradley escorted Anne and CC to the science lab and introduced them to Professor Holloway. "Bradley, so nice to see you again." The professor smiled and shook Bradley's hand. "You were always my favorite student."

"How long ago did you attend Vanderbilt?" Anne asked.

"It was last year. I like to keep up on my studies."

Anne was finding many layers to Bradley. He was quite the onion.

The professor led Anne to the equipment. While the building was old, the lab was modern, stainless steel. Anne felt right at home. This was familiar territory to her. She donned her safety glasses. Bradley put on a lab coat and safety glasses ready to assist. CC watched. Anne crushed the pill into a powder, added nitrating iodine to it and then placed the solution in the IMS.

Bradley adjusted the quadruple mass spectrometer to assure a correct peak assessment. Bradley and Anne looked at each other and nodded. They were in agreement. "It's a placebo, CC," Anne said. "Someone switched Walter's medication with sugar pills."

CC's mouth dropped open. "Why would someone kill Walters? He was destitute and losing everything he had. He didn't even have a place to live," CC said.

"Whoever it was knew about his epilepsy and was

close enough to switch his medication," Anne said, sitting back on the lab stool.

CC sank onto the laboratory stool next to Anne and thought. She thought about everything that had happened from the mugging in the alley to the recent gunshot. She thought about Jenkins. "It wouldn't be enough to have Walters off his medication. You would need a trigger, a catalyst for a seizure." She paused. "A strobe light!"

Chapter Thirty-nine

They pulled up at the Hermitage Hotel. There were several Nashville police cars parked in the valet space, their lights flashing. “That’s strange,” CC said as she handed the keys to the valet. Before the doorman could open the door for them, a uniformed cop grabbed CC by the arm. Detective Clark grabbed her other arm. “What are you doing? What’s going on?” CC tried to pull her arms away.

“We need to question you about the murder of Ricky Jenkins,” Detective Clark said.

“CC, what’s going on?” Anne called, panicked.

“Detective, what do you mean the *murder*?” CC asked, trying to pull herself out of his grasp.

“We responded to a gunshot call at Jenkins’ complex. We found him dead. He was shot in the heart. We found your fingerprints all over the apartment. What were you doing there?” Detective Clark said.

CC grew quiet.

“You purchased a nine millimeter from Franklin Guns yesterday.”

“The gun’s locked up in the safe in my room. I can show it to you if you want,” CC said.

“Please,” The detective said. CC led them to the elevator, the detective keeping a grasp on her arm. They got in the elevator. Anne and Bradley entered the adjacent one. When they got to the ninth floor, CC led the way to their suite. She swiped the key card. “The safe’s right here inside the hall closet.” She opened the double closet doors to find the safe door wide open.

Empty; it had been cleaned out.

Detective Clark pulled out his handcuffs, placed them on her and read her her rights. “This is ridiculous,” CC said. “There’s no evidence. This is purely circumstantial.”

“You might want to speak to your attorney,” Detective Clark said.

“Someone obviously broke into our room and stole the gun. It was here yesterday.” CC turned and looked at Anne. “Anne, they took the tape—the Clarence Riddle tape.”

“I’ll call Nigel, CC. We’ll call an attorney,” Anne called behind her friend as the detective led her back down the hall.

Chapter Forty

CC remained quiet during the short drive to the downtown booking facility. She quietly went through all the procedures. As a journalist, she knew the routines—fingerprinting, mug shots. Anne waited in the outer office after calling Nigel. Bradley who contacted his friend, a prominent Nashville criminal defense attorney.

A female policewoman led CC into a large holding cell. Several women of various sizes talked and laughed as they sat on hard steel benches which surrounded the interior of the cell. CC sat in a corner by herself. She leaned her head against the cold cement wall and closed her eyes. She tried to put the puzzle pieces together. She opened her eyes as she felt someone brush her shoulder. Two large women with short haircuts and bad attitudes had sandwiched CC in between them. Both were covered with tattoos and unpleasant smells. CC tried to stand up. One woman grabbed her by the arm and threw her back on the bench. "That's mighty unfriendly of you," she growled, keeping a grip on CC's arm.

CC did a quick look around the cell to evaluate her chances of surviving an encounter. The black belt in kenpo karate that she'd earned from the Glen Ellyn Park District gave her the confidence not to fight. She'd rather talk her way out of her dilemma. One of the tattooed women said, "We're trying to make you feel comfortable. You look sad. What's wrong? Are you having a bad day?"

The other tattooed woman cackled. As she laughed, CC could see her whittled down yellow teeth, the result of years of smoking crystal meth. Some of the other ladies walked over to join the conversation. CC was now surrounded by a party of six in a space reserved for three. Apparently, CC was the main course. She remembered her kenpo master Koji telling her that the best fight is the one you walk away from. This time when she stood up and the tattooed woman grabbed her arm, CC grabbed the woman by her two fingers and twisted her arm, pushing hard on the pressure point. Then, she slowly lowered the large woman to the floor while the others watched. "I appreciate you wanting to be friends, but you're correct that I've had a bad day and I want to sit quietly. Is that okay?"

The tattooed woman looked up from the floor and nodded, wincing from the pain. The party of six closed in on CC and then suddenly they parted. An older woman with a black crew cut, wearing a cut-off Harley Davidson t-shirt, chinos and studded biker boots stood in front of CC.

CC noticed the motorcycle on the t-shirt was a 1942 knucklehead. "Is that your bike?" she asked. "A lot of people don't appreciate the knucklehead. They want to go with a pan or shovel. The knucklehead is more upkeep but worth the ride."

The biker smiled. "I know you. Are you someone famous? I've seen you somewhere."

The other partygoers stared at CC, also trying to place her. CC noticed that the biker's motorcycle boots were vintage Harley racing boots with worn leather and an early 1960s insignia. "You seem to like vintage motorcycles and gear," CC said. "Have you ever read a blog called the Spoon Sisters?"

The biker woman smiled again. "That's it! That's where I saw your face. Ladies, go sit down. Clear out.

We have a celebrity! Let's give her some room. My name is Marge."

"I'm CC Muller."

"I recognize your name now." Marge sat down next to CC. "Why are you here, CC?"

"I didn't do anything. I'm innocent."

"We're all innocent," Marge said. All the ladies giggled. "Look, CC, you don't have anything to worry about. You're okay. Listen, now that we're friends, maybe you can help me out. I've been looking for a couple parts for my 42."

CC and Marge continued talking into the night. About vintage motorcycles, motorcycle parts, the Nashville police, and diners and dives along Route 66.

In the morning, the guard approached the cell. "Muller," she called. "Come with me." She opened the steel door and CC stepped out.

As she turned the corner, Marge ran up to the bars and waved her over. "Don't forget about the carburetor and the Royal Albert tea set."

"I won't," CC promised. She then followed the guard into the booking room.

"CC, I was so worried about you. I couldn't sleep," Anne said. "Bradley's friend, the attorney, arranged bail. He's going to meet with you later in his office. Nigel's been calling in all his favors to help too."

Chapter Forty-one

After breakfast and a shower, Bradley drove Anne and CC to the attorney's office. His name was Simon Davis and he was way out of CC's price range. She'd read articles about some of his more famous murder trials. Even though he had a high success rate, it seemed that most of his clients should have been found guilty. It made her feel guilty. The tall and handsome Mr. Davis greeted them in the foyer before leading them to his office. "Bradley, good to see you again," he said.

"Good to see you, Simon." The two men shook hands.

CC sat down next to Simon. Anne whispered to Bradley, "How do you know him?"

"Mr. Davis lived at the hotel while he was going through his divorce."

"Oh." Anne nodded. She wondered how much he paid a night to live in the hotel. Maybe there was a special rate for long-term guests.

"Ms. Muller, may I call you CC?"

"Yes, of course."

"I've read through the police report. They found your fingerprints at the crime scene. The victim. . ." Simon paused and shuffled some papers. "Mr. Jenkins was shot with a nine millimeter handgun and apparently the day before, you purchased a nine millimeter." He held up a copy of the sales slip from Franklin Guns.

"It's an antique I bought for one of our clients," CC said, holding her purse primly in her lap.

"We're antique hunters," Anne interjected.

"The police also found gunpowder residue on your jacket when they booked you."

CC laughed; it was so obvious. "I tested the gun at the firing range. Of course, I had gunpowder on my clothes." CC paused. "As soon as I got back to the hotel, I locked the gun in our room safe. I have not opened the safe since. Somebody broke into our room and stole it."

"Who do you believe would do that?" Simon asked.

CC didn't answer.

"How did you know Mr. Jenkins?" he asked.

"He tried to kill me." CC cleared her throat.

"He tried to kill you," Simon repeated, shuffling through his papers again. "There's a police report taken the night of the party at the Hermitage plantation. It states that Mr. Jenkins accidentally fired a dueling pistol that missed you."

"Yes, that's correct," CC said.

"Your fingerprints were found in his apartment after he was found shot with a nine millimeter and you had just purchased a nine millimeter."

"Yes, that's correct," CC repeated.

Simon put the papers down and looked up. "This doesn't look good for you, CC."

"You're missing the larger picture. I believe Jenkins was involved in a conspiracy. I haven't connected all the pieces yet but it involves Blue Note Records, Jenkins, and a recording engineer named Walters," CC said.

Anne reached into her large orange Prada bag and pulled out the prescription bottle. "We found these at West End Studios. That's where Walters was found dead. He drowned in a puddle after an epileptic seizure. We had the pills inside tested. Someone switched out his medication with placebos. We found strobe lights at Jenkins' apartment. I believe he used those to trigger

Walters' seizure."

Simon listened patiently, absorbing the elaborate tale. "Why haven't you brought this to the police?"

"I don't think they'd believe us at this point, would they?" Anne said.

"I will pass this information to my investigator. In the meantime, we've arranged your bail, pending further investigation. There will be a hearing. Don't leave town right now."

"What about your retainer?" CC asked.

"It's been taken care of." Simon looked over at Bradley who nodded.

Anne and CC left the attorney's office and exited the front door of the office building. They stopped at the coffee shop across from the building for a mid-afternoon snack.

"We have to find Lily and tell her about John Lloyd, the producer," CC said, pulling the producer's card out of her wallet.

"CC, we have to prove your innocence," Anne said.

"I don't have to prove I'm innocent. They have to prove I'm guilty. And we both know I'm not guilty."

"Who would try to make you look guilty?" Anne said, biting into her pecan pie with its chocolate syrup drizzle.

"It all leads back to the blue note, starting with Dave Southwell." CC sat back in the booth. "Jenkins was a lighting engineer. Dave Southwell was killed by a spotlight. His roadie had a blue note tattoo like Jenkins, like Walters. The security guard at Dog Ear, Jeffrey, said that Colonel Anderson started Blue Note. I think the next step is we have to talk to the Colonel. First, let's help Lily."

Chapter Forty-two

It was lunchtime and the Listening Room was packed.Anne looked for a table while CC scanned the crowd for the manager. The hallway was filled with flyers advertising upcoming shows and calendar dates, including one for Lily Riddle. They must have really liked her audition. The flyer showed her booked for the next three days. "Excuse me," CC yelled over the chatter. The young red-haired manager walked over. "I'm trying to find Lily Riddle. I'm a friend."

"We haven't seen her. She was supposed to play last night and was a no-show. Right now, I'm trying to find someone to fill in for her tonight in case she doesn't show again," she said.

"Do you have a phone number or address?" CC asked.

"I've tried her phone. There's no answer."

"Thanks," CC said.

Anne waved CC over to a small table. She had ordered fried mac 'n' cheese bites. "Any luck finding Lily?" Anne asked.

CC sat down. "No, she didn't show up last night, and they can't reach her."

Anne took a bite of the mac 'n' cheese. Her mouth burned from the hot, melting cheddar cheese. "Mmm, this is really good. Try some." She pushed the plate toward CC.

CC shook her head.

"What about Brent? Do you want to try him to see if he could find her?" Anne asked.

CC took her iPhone out and dialed Brent. She covered the mouthpiece to be heard over the crowd. And, then hung up. "Brent hasn't seen her."

"I can't believe she would miss this opportunity. She worked so hard to get this chance. She seemed really excited. She's so good."

"Something's not right," CC said.

"Where do we go from here?" Anne asked.

"Everything leads back to Colonel Anderson. We need to talk to him."

"How do we find him?"

"We'll ask Mr. Robertson. He knows the Colonel," CC said, reaching for her phone.

Chapter Forty-three

The crushed stone driveway crackled underneath the VW tires. The rain had started again. It was pitch black in the rural backwoods, thirty miles outside of Nashville. A sign by the Cumberland Bridge read "Caution during heavy rains." They crossed over it carefully. The river was rising. They arrived at the log cabin. They could see the glow of the fire.

Mr. Robertson had told them that the Colonel rarely left his hunting cabin. The lightning flashed, illuminating the driveway. CC pulled the VW over. They got out of the car and ran quickly to the covered porch. The cabin looked like something out of every scary movie they had ever seen.

CC turned the door handle slowly as they slipped inside. The entryway was knotty pine paneling. With flashes of lightning bursting through the windows, they could see the animal heads hanging on the wall, their mouths exposed, baring ferocious teeth. It was a frightening sight. Anne stayed close to CC's back. "What are we doing?" she whispered.

CC didn't answer. She followed the orange, red glow of the only light in the cabin. From the glow of the fire, she could see the back of the Colonel's head as he faced the warmth, a red plaid blanket on his lap. His long white hair flowed over the back of the tall leather wingback chair. She could see his one hand resting on the side table, holding a glass with a drink. *Waterford*, Anne thought. As he lifted the glass, his hand shook.

Some of Anne's anxiety subsided as she trod softly

closer to the chair. "I know you're there. Come sit by the fire. It's a nasty night," the Colonel said.

Anne and CC walked up and sat side by side on the couch facing the Colonel and across from the fireplace. He was wearing thick glasses, his long white beard had not been trimmed in a long time. His face was ashy gray, the skin was paper thin and creviced.

This was not a man long for this world, CC thought.

"You're here about Blue Note, aren't you?"

"Yes, we are," CC said.

"I loved Blue Note like a son."

"What happened to him?"

The Colonel tried to raise his glass again and they could see the wrinkled blue note tattoo on his wrist. His hand shook. Anne got up, held his hand and helped him take a sip. She sat back down. "I never meant for any of this to happen," the Colonel said.

"What happened?" CC asked.

"We were drinking. We all were drinking. It was an accident."

"What was an accident?"

"The bridge. The bridge was an accident."

"What happened at the bridge?"

"They killed my grandfather," said a voice from behind the couch, startling both Anne and CC. Lily walked out of the darkness into the light of the fire. "Walters, the Colonel, Jenkins—they were all there. That night. They killed my grandfather. He wanted to be on stage. He wanted to sing his songs. Instead, they stole his songs."

"She's right. Clarence wrote all the hits. Everybody made money. Everybody shared the wealth. Clarence just cared about the music," the Colonel said. "You have to understand, all the songs he wrote were worth millions of dollars and we were a young company signing all these artists. Gold records, top of the charts, we had it all. It was all because of Clarence."

"Is that why you named the studio after him?" CC asked.

"After he died, we named it Blue Note to honor him," the Colonel said.

"Is that why you all got the blue note tattoo?"

The colonel was quiet. Lily laughed. "It wasn't to honor my grandfather. It was an oath, a pledge. Everyone that was there that night killed my grandfather," she said.

"She's right. We didn't try to stop him," the colonel said. "He was drunk and we kept feeding him drinks. He fell off the Cumberland Bridge and we didn't try to save him. The tattoo." A shaky finger pointed to his wrist and the tattoo. "Everyone that was there that night was guilty. If anyone told what happened, we would all be ruined. No one can give up the other. We all wear the truth on our skin."

"Lily, how'd you find out?" CC asked.

"I called my grandfather after you told me about Clarence. He told me that when he returned from Vietnam looking for his brother, that the Colonel was the only one who helped him. That the Colonel gave him money to start a new life in California. If I ever needed help, I could go to the Colonel."

"Why now?"

Lily sat on the edge of the couch. "After I played the Listening Room, I headed to my apartment. It was late. I'd had a couple drinks. When I went to put the key in my door, someone grabbed me from behind and pulled me down the stairs. I tried to scream. He had his arm around my throat. I couldn't breath. He dragged me along the sidewalk, my boots scraping along the cement. I pulled my boot knife out and stuck him in the leg. He let go of me and I ran. I never went back."

From under his blanket, the Colonel pulled out a

gun. CC recognized it as her nine-millimeter Luger. His hand shook. "I didn't mean for any of this to happen." He put the gun down on the side table. "Clarence was a good man. Dave was a good man," the Colonel said.

"Dave Southwell?" CC asked.

"Dave found out that his songs—the ones we gave him—were all stolen from Clarence. Dave didn't want any part of that. We couldn't have him talk. We couldn't take the chance." The Colonel pointed to his blue note tattoo. "We had to keep the secret. We're a family." He reached into his pocket. With a shaky hand, he pulled the cassette tape out from under the blanket. He looked at it, the tape fell out of his hand. "I didn't want this to happen," he repeated, lifting up his glass of Scotch. The glass dropped and broke. It shattered into pieces on the floor. He gasped for air and coughed. Then, he slumped over. Anne shook him and grabbed his wrist. She put her fingers up to his neck. She looked at CC and shook her head confirming that the Colonel was gone.

Chapter Forty-four

The next morning, Anne and CC sat in the control room at Dog Ear Records listening to Lily sing her grandfather's song. She had written the lyrics for the song she now called, "Cumberland Bridge." The melody and the words were haunting. Brent was playing electric guitar behind her. Anne leaned in toward CC. "You know, he looks like a young Brad Pitt; you know, like in Thelma and Louise."

"Quiet, just quiet." CC said.

"If he's a young Brad Pitt, that would make you Thelma," she giggled.

Lily finished the song and came out to the control room.

"You sounded great, Lily," CC said. "I spoke to my attorney. His firm is going to represent you. Your grandfather got cheated out of a lot of money. The royalties for all his hit songs should go to you."

"Thank you so much," Lily said.

Brent followed Anne and CC outside to where the VW bus was waiting. Anne got in the car. CC leaned her back against the bus. Brent pulled in close to her and took her in his arms. "I guess you're heading back to Chicago," he said.

CC nodded.

Brent kissed her. CC kissed him back. She jumped in the VW. Anne mumbled, "Thelma."

"What? What did you say?" CC asked.

"Nothing."

Anne and CC left the studio and headed back to the

Hermitage. Anne headed up to the room to finish packing. CC wandered around the hotel. She stopped in the fitness room. She realized she had not worked out once since leaving Chicago. It was a nice room with four treadmills, free weights, and a universal weight machine. On a bench press in the corner, she saw Bradley wearing sweatpants and a t-shirt that read Army. During her whole stay at the Hermitage, she had never seen Bradley in anything other than his uniform. She counted the weights on the barbell over his head and was amazed to see him bench pressing three hundred pounds.

The hotel manager walked by, stopping to speak to CC. "Ms. Muller, I have your bill ready for you at the front desk."

CC followed him to the front desk. She took a look around, did a 360 to soak in the elegant lobby one last time. She had not appreciated it as much as Anne had but she was sorry now that they had to leave. Until she looked at the bill.

At her surprised look, the manager said, "We did give you the media rate."

"Oh, no; I'm sure it's right, and we've had a wonderful stay here," CC said. "I can't say enough wonderful things about Bradley. He's really amazing."

"We're very lucky to have Bradley. He's been with us for forty years," the manager said. "He joined us after he left the army. He started as a bellboy."

"I saw him bench pressing 300 pounds. He's got to be what about 70?"

The manager nudged her closer. CC stretched over the marble counter. "Bradley was a Green Beret. Part of the fifth Special Forces. The most decorated Special Forces group in U.S. history. He never speaks of it, but my father worked here when Bradley started. They were bellboys together. Bradley's team was responsible for recon missions in Cambodia. Bradley received the medal of honor."

CC pulled back, nodded and stood upright. "It all makes sense now."

Anne walked up behind her, followed by several bellboys pushing rolling luggage racks. "Where's Bradley? No one's seen Bradley. I have to say goodbye," Anne said.

CC settled the bill. The bellboys loaded up the VW bus. Anne waited on the steps, staring up at the beautiful exterior. It was painful to say goodbye. The door swung open and Bradley appeared in his uniform, holding a basket. "Miss Hillstrom, one last lunch. I've packed you something special for the ride home," he said.

"Oh, Bradley," Anne said with a quivering voice. Her eyes started watering. "Bradley, I wish we could stay forever." He held the car door open for her. "I'm going to miss you." She paused and gave him a hug.

Bradley tapped her lightly on the back, looking embarrassed.

"Oh, Bradley." Anne hugged him again. "I really don't want to leave."

CC rolled her eyes.

Chapter Forty-five

Anne adjusted her pink-flowered Adrianna Papell silk suit bought at a bargain price on eBay as she followed CC off the elevator into the Signature Room on the 95th floor in Chicago's John Hancock Building. Betsy had reserved the entire restaurant for her engagement party, and Anne wanted to do the setting justice. She looked marvelous if she thought so herself. She paused to admire her reflection in the mirror across from the elevator.

CC stood next to her adjusting her perfect little black dress. Combined with her pearls, it made a perfect statement.

They walked into the entryway of the restaurant and lounge. The floor to ceiling windows showcased the Chicago skyline and lakefront. The lights from the buildings glowed an incandescent yellow. From this height, the buildings looked like a city made of Legos. Anne pressed her nose against the window. The headlights of the cars driving up and down Michigan Avenue appeared to be one continuous line of light. Anne thought about the stores along the Magnificent Mile. At this time, they would be closed. That was okay; they had spent the day shopping and the car was overflowing with her purchases.

Anne thought, *God Forbid, there was an earthquake! All the beautiful people of Chicago are in one room tonight. How would the city survive?* She laughed to herself.

Wearing a stunning silver sequined Aidan Mattox

long gown with a train, Betsy swirled up to them. *Neiman Marcus*, Anne thought, *way beyond her price range. Definitely this season, if not next. Betsy had spared no expense for this party.* "Anne! CC!" Betsy hugged them both at the same time, holding her champagne glass way out. "So glad you could make it!" She brushed her cheek against Anne and then CC at a safe distance from possibly smearing her lipstick. *First name basis, we must have done good,* Anne thought.

"The coach house is magnificent. I love every piece that you found and Steven loves it, too. He wants to thank you himself. He's running late," Betsy said, glancing around the room.

The party continued with music, champagne and appetizers. CC mingled with a group from the Art Institute, giving a lecture on French Impressionism to the curator responsible for the Monet exhibit on loan from the Louvre. She accented her points in her schoolgirl French. The Paris-born curator smiled politely, not wanting to correct her.

Anne perused the buffet. She had given herself one last night off from her diets. She piled a plate high with the remaining crab legs. It was getting late, and the party was slowing down. Anne looked out the window at the stars over the city. It was beautiful. Michigan Avenue was deserted. It looked peaceful from 95 stories up. Anne thought about Bradley and the Hermitage.

"The Art Institute curator invited me to the exclusive premier," CC said, walking up behind Anne.

Betsy came up to them. "I'm glad you're still here. Steven just showed up. His flight was delayed." She called, "Steven!" and waved him over to them.

"Ladies, good to see you." He walked up to them and put his arm around Betsy's waist.

"Congratulations," CC said.

"Thanks for inviting us," Anne said, grabbing a shrimp puff from the waiter as he walked by. As he tried to continue his walk, she pulled him back and grabbed the last one.

Steven walked away to say goodbye to the last guests. It was after 3 a.m., and the staff was getting anxious to leave too. "I'm glad he made it back in time," Betsy said. "With the funeral arrangements."

"What funeral arrangements?" CC asked.

"Steven's grandfather passed away."

"I'm so sorry to hear that," CC said.

"I never met him. I know he was very old and in poor health so it wasn't a shock. He gave Steven his start in the business." Betsy's voice dropped to a theatrical whisper. "Steven doesn't talk much about it. He wants people to think he's self-made, but his grandfather mentored him. He also funded his first business. He owes everything to the Colonel."

"The Colonel?" Anne and CC asked in unison.

"Steven's grandfather was Colonel Anderson. He was Steven's maternal grandfather," Betsy continued. "After Steven's father died, he went to live with the Colonel. The Colonel raised him. They even have matching tattoos."

"Tattoo?" CC asked.

"What about my grandfather?" Steven said, walking up behind them.

"I was telling them about your grandfather." Betsy put a manicured hand on Steven's sleeve.

Steven stared quietly at Anne and CC. "The ladies met my grandfather when they were in Nashville."

"Oh, that's nice," Betsy said. "Oh, the manager is waving to me. Excuse me." She sashayed off.

CC grabbed Anne's arm. "We have to go."

"I just got here. You can't leave now. We have to catch up," Steven said.

"We're not feeling well," Anne replied.

Walking backwards to the elevator, they pressed the down button. CC tapped her foot with a growing sense of urgency. The 40-second wait for the elevator to speed from the first floor to the 95th seemed like hours. Anne held CC's hand. Her eyes closed. She was breathing heavily. "What are we going to do? What about Betsy?"

Exiting the building, they headed to the street that led behind Michigan Avenue. CC had found a low-priced parking lot off of Lower Walker Drive. It was cheaper than parking in the adjacent parking garage off Michigan Avenue.

They walked down the stairs leading to the grimy parking lot. During the day, they had felt safe while they shopped but now the stores were closed and no one was out. It was a world of shadows and unfamiliar noises. They reached the bottom of the metal steps. CC grabbed Anne and whispered, "Quiet." They could hear the click of heavy footsteps coming down the stairs behind them. "Run, Anne!" They ran down the narrow alley, avoiding the potholes. CC slipped and fell on her knees. Anne picked her up by the arm. They made it to the VW, jumped in and clicked all the door-lock buttons shut.

CC fumbled for her keys in her purse. She dropped them on the floor. She knelt down to find them. When she got up, she could see a large figure in the rearview mirror running with a limp toward the bus. The VW started with a poof. The engine cranked and then turned over. CC threw it in reverse almost hitting the dark figure who jumped out of their way.

"Hurry, CC! Drive!" Anne shouted, panting.

As CC squealed out of the parking lot, she could see headlights following behind her. She drove up the ramp leading to Michigan Avenue, doing 50 miles an hour.

She flew through the red light, swerving onto the street, which was empty. She headed south. The little VW engine strained, pushing 55, 56 miles an hour. CC floored the pedal. Anne turned around in her seat looking out the back window watching the headlights getting closer. The big Ford F250 lights were bearing down on them. "Hurry, CC! He's getting close!" Anne said, clutching her evening bag. She reached into it and pulled out her phone. She dialed Nigel. There was no answer, but she screamed into his voicemail, ""It's Anne. We're going be killed! We're on Michigan Avenue. Please help us!"

She lost her signal. She tried dialing 911. "CC, I can't get a signal."

"Keep trying," CC said as they reached the Michigan Avenue Bridge. The VW hit 70 miles per hour and that's when the truck slammed into it, pushing the bus sideways and up and onto the railing.

The 1968 Volkswagen Bus teetered over the Michigan Avenue Bridge. On one side, certain death; on the other, really great shopping. Anne reached over the passenger seat and into the back to grab her bags. "That bag has my vintage Orrefors wine decanter," she said. "I've spent years searching for it."

"Anne, don't move," CC cautioned.

Anne ignored her friend, and the bus tipped closer to certain death than to shopping. She crawled to the back of the bus to save her day's worth of finds. As she did, the bus teetered back towards the bridge, rising up slowly.

For once, CC couldn't give her a hard time about going off her diet. This time it paid off. "Anne, stay where you are. Don't move." CC crawled back by Anne and the bus leveled out.

"What do we do now?"

“When I open the back window, we both have to crawl out at the same time,” CC said.

The Ford F250 idled in the middle of the street. The engine revved. And then the tires squealed and rammed into the rear of the bus. The bus slid, catching its back tires on the rails, the only thing keeping the bus from falling in the river. Anne and CC tumbled back into the front of the bus. CC crawled into the driver’s seat.

Anne looked up from the floor. “Look at my dress. It’s ruined.”

CC smiled. She loved her old friend. She reached down and helped her back into her seat.

“This is it. We’re going to die, aren’t we?” Anne said in a quivering voice.

CC didn’t answer and took her hand in hers. They both looked down into the cold dark of the Chicago River. Then the back window crashed in. An arm brandishing a gun came through the window. They could see the light blue of the quarter note tattoo shining in the moonlight.

Anne crawled up toward the back of the bus. Her skirt caught on the armrest, tearing.

“What are you doing?” CC yelled.

Anne climbed over the bags and boxes, clinging to the side of the VW, reaching for any hold she could grasp. She slipped a bit and then caught a hand again, pulling herself up with all her remaining strength. Taking the Orrefors vase out of the box, she dangled, holding on one with hand and with the other smashed the gun out of his hand. The vase shattered, sending shards of crystal deep into his arm. He screamed.

Then he stuck his head into the window, Anne reached around to push him away. He stuck his head in again and his ponytail caught on the jagged glass, snapping his head back. He yelled, “You just won’t die!

Jenkins couldn't kill you at the falls or in the alley. You made me kill Jenkins. Now I have to kill you!"

Anne reached around the van looking for a weapon. She saw the gun lodged against the side panel at the same time Roger did. She couldn't reach it and she was losing her hold, starting to slide back. Roger pushed his way through the window, his ponytail starting to tear. His fingers inches away from the revolver. Anne looked down and saw her large orange Prada bag. She grabbed it and felt around inside. She touched the soft eagle feather. She pulled it out and stabbed Roger, the roadie, in the eye with the pointed quill. He screamed and fell backward onto the pavement, leaving his ponytail dangling from the jagged glass. He rolled on the ground in agonizing pain.

"Anne, we have to get out of here," CC said as the VW groaned and squealed, metal scraping against metal. She pulled herself up toward Anne. She unlatched the window that swung out.

"Anne, you have to move a little," CC said as they both tried to exit the window at the same time.

"CC, I'm stuck. I'm not going to fit."

CC glanced behind Anne and noticed that she was holding her large orange Prada bag along with several shopping bags. "What are you doing? Let go of the bags."

"*My* bags!"

"Anne, you have to let go of the bags. You're not going to fit through the window with those bags. You have to let it go."

At Anne's panicked look, CC touched her cheek and in a calm, quiet voice said, "Anne, just let it go."

Anne thought about it and realized CC was right. She pushed through the window, making one last grab, pulled the large orange Prada bag to safety. She held it up triumphantly. They heard the death rattle of the VW as the tires gave way, sending it plunging toward the Chicago River. Their last glimpse of the bus before it entered its watery grave was the bumper sticker that read, “The Spoon Sisters.”

Anne and CC lay on the cool cement of the Michigan Avenue bridge walkway as the fire department and police arrived. Roger, the roadie, rolled on the ground, grabbing his face. Blood dripped from his eye.

The EMTs put him into the waiting ambulance. Another EMT walked over and put blankets on both Anne and CC. He took their vitals. “Are you ladies, okay?”

They both shook their heads, still breathing hard. Nigel rushed up to them. “Anne, are you all right? What happened? I came as soon as I got your message.”

He knelt down. Anne put her arms around his neck and pulled him close. “Nigel, I was so scared.” She told him the story about Blue Note Records, the Colonel and Steven. Nigel relayed the story to his commander who sent a squad to the Signature Room to arrest Steven.

Chapter Forty-six

After finishing breakfast, CC sat down at the table to blog, "Dear Friends, I'm sorry it's been a while since I've written."

Anne sat next to her picking at the plate of Danish. She deserved an additional treat after her ordeal. Her one more day off her diet had turned into another one more day.

"So much has happened. I've attached the *Chicago Tribune* article that I wrote. It's my first byline in a major newspaper," she wrote, smiling. "It tells about the bridge and the Blue Note murders, all of our recent ordeals," CC continued typing. A chat window opened on her screen with a shrill noise. It was Betsy. "Hi Betsy," CC said.

"Hi, Betsy." Anne stood in the background, peering over CC's shoulder.

"Where are you?" CC asked.

"I'm at O'Hare. I'm heading to Paris. I'm going to be gone for a while. I wanted to say goodbye." Betsy paused, pushing her Fendi sunglasses up onto her forehead.

"I'm so sorry everything turned out like it did," CC said.

"Me too," Betsy said, showing an expressionless face. She paused, trying to think of something to say. "I have to go. They're boarding my plane." Betsy pressed off and disappeared.

"You think Betsy will be okay?" Anne asked.

"Betsy's always fine," CC said.

"You notice she was wearing the cashmere trench coat from Burberry. I don't even think it's available here yet. She's probably going to all the runway shows." Anne pictured herself strolling on the Champs-Ėlysées, arms loaded with one-of-a-kind designer originals and enjoying pastries at a sidewalk café. "Mmm, petit fours." She eyed the Danish again with disdain. It was the lesser cousin of the French pastry. "I wish I could fly off on a whim and go to Paris," she said, biting off a piece of the cheese sweet roll.

Not answering, CC returned to her blog; her fans were waiting. Anne looked around for her phone to check her eBay watch list. "CC, have you seen my phone?" Anne dug into her large orange Prada bag. She pulled out an envelope. It had the Cherokee casino logo on it.

"What's that?" CC asked.

"I forgot about this. John Blackbear gave it to me." Anne turned it over. "Maybe it's a gift card for a free stay at the casino. That would be fun."

CC continued writing.

Anne ripped open the envelope. The check read, "Pay to the order of Anne Hillstrom, $250,000."

"CC, how do you feel about Paris?" Anne asked.

THE END

RECIPES

CC's Frittata

Cream
Eggs
Vegetables, such as onions, mushrooms, sautéed
Salt
Pepper

Beat eggs and slowly add heavy cream. Add vegetables of your choosing. You can also add any meat or cheese. Add salt and pepper to taste. Dash of ghost pepper optional. Place in cast iron skillet. Bake in oven at 350 degrees for 30 minutes. Serve with sliced strawberries and fresh mint leaves.

CC's Shrimp Scampi

1 pound shrimp, peeled and deveined
fresh minced garlic
Olive oil
Lemon juice
Basil
Splash of vermouth

Sautee shrimp in fresh garlic, olive oil. Add splash of lemon juice. Garnish with basil. Just before finished, add splash of vermouth. Drizzle olive oil, salt, pepper and parmesan on romaine. Grill until edges are crispy. Place romaine on plate, add shrimp. Sprinkle with feta. Add a slice of watermelon. Optional blueberry vinaigrette

Hot Brown

Slices of turkey, roast beef
Toast
Cream, cheddar cheese
Parmesan
Tomato
Bacon

Melt cheddar cheese with cream and butter until a smooth consistency. Top toast with slices of roast beef and turkey. Place cheddar cheese mixture on top. Add slice of bacon and tomato. Sprinkle with parmesan. Grill until crispy.

CC's Pain Perdu

Five eggs
½ cup white sugar
½ cup milk
Orange liqueur
Orange zest

Beat eggs, sugar and milk until frothy. Add orange liqueur and orange zest. Cut bread into twelve slices. Soak the bread slices in the egg mixture for 2 minutes on each side. Melt butter in griddle and heat to medium. Cook bread slices in griddle for 2 minutes on each side or until they are golden brown. Drizzle warm maple syrup on top. Garnish with fresh orange slice.

ABOUT THE AUTHOR

With a passion for shopping, Vicki Vass drew on her experiences as an antique hunter to tell the story of her real-life friends Anne and CC. This book is the second in their series. The first was entitled MURDER BY THE SPOONFUL.

Vicki Vass has written more than 1,400 articles for *The Chicago Tribune* as well as *Women's World*, *The Daily Herald* and *Home & Away*. Her science fiction novel, *The Lexicon,* was inspired by her journeys in the jungle of Sudan, Africa, while writing about the ongoing civil war for World Relief.

She lives outside Chicago, with her writer, musician, husband Brian, their 20-year old son Tony, kittens Pixel and Terra, Australian shepherd Bandit, seven koi and Gary the turtle.